Y FICTION KIM

Kimmel, Elizabeth Cody.

Unhappy medium

Please check all items for damages
before leaving the Library.
Thereafter you will be held
responsible for all injuries
to items beyond reasonable wear.

Helen M. Plum Memorial Library

Lombard, Illinois

A daily fine will be charged for
overdue materials.

AUG   2011

Suddenly Supernatural

UNHAPPY MEDIUM

by

Elizabeth Cody Kimmel

LITTLE, BROWN AND COMPANY

Books for Young Readers

New York   Boston

Copyright © 2009 by Elizabeth Cody Kimmel

Little, Brown Books for Young Readers

Hachette Book Group
237 Park Avenue, New York, NY 10017
Visit our Web site at www.lb-kids.com

Little, Brown Books for Young Readers is a division of Hachette Book Group, Inc. The Little, Brown name and logo are trademarks of Hachette Book Group, Inc.

First Edition: April 2009

Kimmel, Elizabeth Cody.
Unhappy medium / by Elizabeth Cody Kimmel. — 1st ed.
p. cm. — (Suddenly supernatural)
Summary: Kat accompanies her best friend, Jac, to a musicians' conference at the Whispering Pines Mountain House, where she works to free the spirit of a dead medium and helps Jac resolve a serious conflict.
ISBN 978-0-316-06687-7
[1. Spiritualists — Fiction. 2. Haunted places — Fiction. 3. Supernatural — Fiction. 4. Hotels, motels, etc. — Fiction. 5. Mothers and daughters — Fiction. 6. Friendship — Fiction.] I. Title.
PZ7.K56475Un 2009
[Fic] — dc22
2008045021

10 9 8 7 6 5 4 3 2 1

RRD-C

Printed in the United States of America

The text was set in RuseX, and the display type is AT Raphael

Suddenly Supernatural

UNHAPPY MEDIUM

Chapter 1

I daydream a lot, especially during science class. I can dream up the perfect dessert, the perfect day, the perfect slice of pizza, even the perfect boy. But I have to tell you, sleeping or awake I could never have imagined a place that looked like the Whispering Pines Mountain House.

My best friend Jac's mother was a painfully slow driver, so it seemed to be taking forever to get closer to the hotel itself. But eventually she managed to pull the car into the circular drive by the main entrance.

Almost immediately, a guy in a red-and-black uniform and an embarrassing little cap approached our car.

"Checking in?" he asked. And he glanced at the backseat at me and Jac and gave us a little wink. Now that's what I call service.

"Yes," replied Mrs. Gray, a little icily. "We're with the Young Northeast Musician's Convention."

Jac's mother is not exactly the warm and fuzzy type. I'm betting in a previous life she was Attila the Hun, or some other big guy with a spear that scared everybody half to death and ate raw meat.

Jac leaned close to me and whispered. "Kat, what do you think? A place like this has to be seething with ghosts, doesn't it?"

I didn't quite take to the concept of *seething with ghosts.* But Whispering Pines was built in the mid-1800s, and it was enormous.

As one of the oldest hotels in the northeast, the place was certain to be filled with spirits, and I was betting some of them were going to be very happy to see me. What's worse, I was betting some of them *weren't*.

I didn't ask to be a medium. It just happened. Apparently it runs in the family. My mom says if I ever have a child of my own, chances are fifty-fifty that on the kid's thirteenth birthday they'll start seeing spooks, too. Then there will be three consecutive generations of us who can communicate with the dead. If I have triplets, we could start our own spirit-seeing volleyball team. Imagine the possibilities!

"Girls, I'm going to go inside and get us checked in. Why don't you stay here with our things until I'm done?"

It wasn't really a question. Jac and I nodded, and Mrs. Gray stepped out of the car and walked primly toward the entrance. As usual, she was dressed like she'd just come from a reception at the White House.

"She seriously thinks the bellboy might rip off some of our stuff if we leave the car unattended," Jac said. "I'm sure her collection of tweeds and velvet headbands would cause a virtual stampede on eBay."

"I think it's your cello that she's worried about," I said.

"Well, that makes two of us," Jac muttered, staring out the window.

After the huge deal Jac had made about quitting the cello just two months ago, I was as surprised as everyone else when she started playing again. Secretly, I was pleased, but I tried not to make too much out of it. I knew Jac well enough to know that if and when she wanted to talk, she'd let me know.

I examined her profile. Her red hair was

pulled back with a silver barrette, exposing one tiny ear, and her eyebrows were furrowed.

"Are you okay?" I asked. "Having second thoughts?"

Jac shrugged.

I remained silent. There was nothing I could say that would help the hopelessly complicated relationships that Jac had with her mother, and with her cello. Jac was incredibly gifted — there was no doubt about that. But after a lifetime of being pushed to excel at her music, Jac had rebelled.

Mrs. Gray had spent the last two months trying to lure Jac back to her musical studies. When she pitched the idea of attending the weeklong YNMC convention at the famous Whispering Pines Mountain House, Jac agreed — under one condition.

I had to be invited, too.

"Let's at least get out of the car," Jac said. "I want to smell the mountain air. I don't think the cello-thieving bellboy will try to make a move if we're standing right here."

I agreed with a giggle, and we climbed out of the SUV, which was the size of a small hut. I think Mrs. Gray thought it was safer to drive a ginormous car.

"This will be so worth it," Jac said, taking my arm. "Look at this place. Look at that *lake*! There are supposed to be hiking trails all over the place, and you can take boats out on the water. I even heard there's a labyrinth in one of the gardens. I've never been in one, have you?"

I shook my head, pleased to see Jac looking so animated.

"And the best thing, Kat, the reason I agreed to come, is that none of the YNMC stuff is required. You show up to what you want, when you want. And the parents have their own meetings, so they can't play prison warden 24–7. No pressure, for once. We'll have plenty of time for some *adventures*."

She whispered the last word, and I knew that the adventures Jac most wanted were of the supernatural kind. Though Jac had an almost pathological fear of everything from yellow-jackets to food poisoning, she had a hearty interest in the spirit world. Her enthusiasm had not been thwarted by the mega-haunted house we'd explored over spring break or by the ghost of the miserable flute player who'd haunted the school library. I had chosen my best friend wisely, because I had come to learn all too well that spirits flocked to me like moths to a flame.

As we waited for Jac's mom to return, enjoying the sun on our faces, my eye was drawn to a figure approaching on my right.

She was a very tall, heavyset woman of a grandmotherly age with a severe face and a constricting Victorian outfit of long full skirts and a cinched-in waist. She walked regally with a serious sense of purpose and was surrounded by an electric flicker that only the alternately energetically abled can achieve. Dead, you know. So I wasn't even in the door yet and I'd seen my first ghost.

Chapter 2

Jac's mother came out to get us, turning over the luggage and the keys to her monster SUV to the bellboy with obvious reluctance.

"We're on the fifth floor," she said, casting a suspicious last look at the bellboy over one shoulder as we walked inside. And she handed me something brass colored, attached to a tag.

"Here's your key, Katherine. An actual key, if such a thing provides any security these days. How archaic."

My mom and I didn't travel much, but

even I knew that most hotels used plastic key cards to open doors. I loved the old brass key, which felt cold and heavy in my hand as we waited for the elevator. My room number was 505 — easy enough to remember.

The official plan was that Jac and her mother would share one room, and I would have another. So not cool, and Jac and I decided not to mention this little detail to my mom. Anyway, Jac was already plotting to modify this arrangement — her theory being that her mother would agree to anything to keep her at the music conference now that we'd arrived. She shot me a knowing look as the ancient creaking elevator arrived.

We rode the elevator up five floors in silence. Jac's mother clutched the railing on the back of the car, white knuckled, and I have to admit the elevator did seem a little shaky. As it lurched along, Jac's hand shot out and she grabbed onto the railing, too. The sight of both Mrs. Gray and Jac hanging on almost cracked me up. I guess Jac inherited her anxieties directly from her mom. To me, this was like wearing a seat belt in an airplane. If the thing goes down, you're toast either way.

The hallway on the fifth floor was dimly lit and heavily carpeted. Everything was super plush, highly polished and slightly musty — "Victorian chic," as I'd seen it described on a blog review of the Mountain House. I much preferred it to the Pleasantview Motor Inn my mom and I stayed in last year for our one glorious day of room service and indoor swimming. Family vacation, Roberts-style.

Our rooms were at the end of the hall, facing one another. Jac grinned wildly at me and waggled her eyebrows up and down while her mother fumbled with the key to room 504.

"I'll be over soon," she mouthed, and I nodded and slipped the key to room 505 in the keyhole. It turned smoothly and the door opened with a low-pitched creak. I walked into the room, shutting the door behind me. It was big, with a double bed, an enormous wardrobe, and a door that opened onto a little porch with a lake view. I crossed to the window and looked out at the water, sighing with happiness. This was the perfect way to start the summer. I loved Whispering Pines Mountain House already.

I was turning around to go inspect the bathroom and see what kind of free stuff was in there when I found my way blocked.

It was the large, imposing woman I'd seen outside.

Instinctively I jumped back, because we were practically nose to, well, collarbone, and mumbled "sorry."

The woman's eyebrows shot up.

"Yes, I can see you," I said. There wasn't any point in waiting to be asked.

The woman looked to the left, then to the right, then back at me. She looked as if, I'm sorry to say, *she'd* seen a ghost. Her mouth dropped open in frank astonishment. The shawl that she had around her shoulders dropped to the floor on one side. Automatically, she reached up and pulled it back over her arm, never letting her eyes leave mine.

Okay. This one wasn't going to be easy. But that didn't mean she had to be difficult.

"I can see you," I repeated, slowly and deliberately. "Is there some way that I can help you?"

The woman took a step back, and her gaze intensified. Very slowly, she began to smile.

"Can I help you?" I repeated, because frankly the Victorian specter was starting to get on my nerves. Did she speak English?

"Success," the woman whispered, her eyes widening. "I have lifted the veil! Lifted the veil!"

What? Did the woman think I was a bride or something?

"Excuse me, I don't understand," I said.

"I knew that with patience ... you are here at last! I have summoned you!" the woman proclaimed triumphantly.

I sighed. Spirits were often muddled. They didn't know what year it was, or where they were, and they sometimes mistook you for someone else. I was getting used to it. But this was *my* room — I had to sleep here.

So the Victorian lady and I needed to get our ducks in a row.

"Okay. Now is there something you need?"

You have to ask, because sometimes spirits are wandering around their old haunts, so to speak, because they enjoy it. They're attached to something about the place, and they return to it frequently. Like comfort food. Not all ghosts were wandering around tormented and confused and unable to cross over to the other side. Those just seemed to be the ones I attracted.

The woman raised both hands in the air in a biblical-looking gesture.

"Madame Serena triumphs! Detractors and skeptics will laugh no more. The Colonel's wife will be vindicated. You are here, as clear as day. I see you as you see me."

I nodded, tapping my foot a little and resisting the impulse to look at my watch. You couldn't just tell a ghost to get on with it. She'd tell me what she wanted when she was good and ready.

She *looked* good and ready. She took a step toward me and opened her mouth so wide I could see her phantom tonsils.

"I command you," she cried, "to *do my will!*"

Oh for Pete's sake, I thought.

But my irritation was interrupted by a loud knock on the door.

"Excuse me for a sec," I said, crossing to the door.

I peered out through the peephole and saw the bellboy from check-in, holding my old suitcase in a neatly gloved hand.

Great. A cute boy knocking on my door, and I've got six feet of dead Victorian drama queen looming over my shoulder. Very appealing to guys, I'm sure.

I shot a glance back at Madame Serena, who was standing up so straight and breathing in so deeply it looked like she was about to launch into an ear-splitting, operatic solo.

I yanked the door open and stood in the doorway, blocking the bellboy's view of the room. My stance seemed to perplex him.

"Where would you like this?" he asked, after a moment.

"Yes," I said.

He went from looking confused to looking a little alarmed.

"I mean, anywhere inside is fine," I corrected.

He hesitated again.

"Excuse me, but . . . um . . ." he said, his voice hesitant, as he tried to look around me and into the room.

Oh no. He'd seen her. She was almost a foot taller than me and half again as wide. Now what?

"Excuse me, I can't get by with you standing there," he said.

Oh.

I stepped aside and he pulled my bag into the room, as if the Victorian woman wasn't there. Which I suppose technically was true. She, on the other hand, was giving him an outraged glare.

I nodded, then gulped as the bellboy walked straight through the back of the lady and out the other side. He deposited my bag at the foot of the bed, and extended one gloved hand, palm up, toward me as he glanced at the floor.

Did he want me to high-five him?

It wasn't until I saw the Victorian lady fumbling in her purse that I realized the bellboy was waiting for a tip. Apparently some traditions are timeless. I reached in my jeans pocket, pulled out a mushed and slightly damp dollar bill, and put it in his hand.

"Thank you!" he said smartly, then quickly strode out of the room, closing the door behind him.

He wouldn't be so thankful when he opened his palm and saw there was only one measly, yucky dollar there that would probably leave a little stain on his glove. But what could I do? I hadn't been prepared.

With the bellboy gone, my gaze returned to the Victorian lady, and I remembered again that she was waiting for me to do her will.

Fat chance.

"I think you may be a little confused," I said, keeping my tone as polite as possible.

She drew herself up to her full height. The sight was intimidating. Seriously, for all the frills and lace and feminine little bows on her outfit, the woman resembled a linebacker.

"I have been more than patient," the woman said, her voice wavering dramatically. "I have endured the waves of skepticism — I have listened to them brand me a fraud and a charlatan. The fox would have destroyed us all. But now, after so long, you have come. We have much work to do, spirit!"

Spirit? Fox? Did this have something to do with the bride and her veil?

I had to proceed carefully. Clearly, this was one of those ghosts who was operating under a misconception. Put simply, she didn't realize she was dead. This was complicated by the fact that she apparently believed I was the one who'd died.

I'm going to go out on a limb and guess

that you've never had the experience of having to inform someone that they're dead. And I hope you never do. It's a tricky business. I know this more from hearing about my mother's experiences than having had my own. I'm still pretty new at this.

The way Mom tells it, learning they're no longer among the living doesn't exactly strike many folks as good news. Ghosts do a wide variety of things when they're mad. According to my mom, their reactions can range from hurling furniture to turning the room into a virtual freezer. They could wreak havoc through the electrical systems, or drive you nuts by hiding your stuff. They could make sudden loud noises and turn you into a nervous wreck. They could appear out of thin air and hover in front of you. They could invade your dreams. Maybe worse.

I wasn't too keen on any of this stuff

happening, though if forced to choose, I might go with the turning the room into a freezer. The cold had never bothered me much, and I had packed a well-worn and comfortable sweatshirt.

"I can try to help you," I told the woman again. "But you have to want to be helped. Did you say your name was Madame Serena?"

She placed one hand to her chest, half closed her eyes, and nodded. Like just admitting she was Madame Serena was a major emotional event. This lady was Very. Highly. Dramatic. I decided maybe I should postpone the little news flash about her being dead, in the hopes that I could find out something about who she was and why she was connected to Whispering Pines. I mean really, how many Madame Serenas could there be?

Chapter 3

I took a deep breath

"Okay, Madame Serena. I am Kat."

"A cat!" the woman whispered. "The spirit world has sent me an animal guide — excellent! Are you a leopard? A cougar? Tell me, spirit — are you a jaguar?"

I suspected that in the mid-nineteenth century someone had filled Madame Serena's head with a load of hooey.

"I'm not a jaguar," I said, hearing how ridiculous it sounded to my own ears. "It's a name, okay? That's all. It's simple. Kaaaaaat,"

I said, drawing the name out like she was a very young, hard-of-hearing child who spoke only Portuguese.

"But of course!" she whispered. "I have been told of Indian guides remaining in the astral realms to assist the incarnate. I am honored to meet you, Simple Cat."

"I'm not . . . my name isn't . . . there are a few things you are not understanding correctly. I'm . . . I come from . . ."

"The Gates of Horn!" Madame Serena cried, clapping her hands together.

"Upstate New York, actually," I corrected. "What I'm trying to say is that I come from another . . ."

"Dimension! Valhalla, the Great Unknown, the Realm of Golden Suchness!"

". . . from another time," I finished.

Madame Serena closed her eyes and tilted her head back.

"The Time of No Time, which is its own beginning, and its own end," she whispered reverently.

I sighed. This was the slowest dead person I'd encountered in my very brief career as a medium. I needed to unpack, and I had to use the bathroom. I should just blurt out the truth and get it over with. If Madame Serena turned out to be a furniture hurler, maybe I could ask for a different room.

"Madame Serena —," I began, but I was interrupted by another knock on the door.

"Now that you have come, there is much we must accomplish. We meet here tonight," Madame Serena said excitedly. "We will form the circle for all who request help, and I will call for you. Come to me in the circle, Simple Cat, and we will begin our work."

The knock sounded again.

"Kat?" I heard Jac's muffled voice through the thick door. "Come on, open up!"

"I don't think this is going to work the way you think it will," I said. "You're not understanding. And I've got to open the door."

Madame Serena clasped her hands together and beamed.

"Yes, Simple Cat. You must open the door between the worlds. You are the Guardian of the Sacred Portal of Transmigration."

I shook my head in frustration, crossed to the door, and opened it to reveal Jac's beaming face. She stood on her tippy toes to look over my shoulder.

"I heard that!" she said excitedly, pushing past me and walking into my room as I shut the door behind her.

"You were talking to someone," Jac

said triumphantly. "Your room is haunted, isn't it?"

Great. Jac has just inadvertently tipped off Madame Serena to the possibility that she was a ghost. But a quick glance showed that Madame Serena was gone. Apparently she'd said what she wanted to say. For such a large lady, she'd sure made a quick exit.

"Well, Maestra, as a matter of fact it is," I told Jac, and she gave a little whoop of excitement.

"I knew it! Tell me everything! Who is it? Were you scared? Was it a woman in white wringing her hands and wailing? That show *Real Afterlife* had an episode about a hotel haunted by a woman in white wringing her hands and wailing. Did you see something right away? Did the room get cold? Was there a murder? Or was it someone who died for love?"

The rolling shade on the window suddenly snapped up with a clatter. Jac shrieked, and jumped about a foot.

"Jac, it's just a shade. I think you need to cut back on the *Real Afterlife* marathons."

"No way, it's the best show ever!" Jac exclaimed. "Way more fun than *Celebrity Shoplifters*. So who's doing the haunting? What's their deal?"

"A woman. An older woman. Victorian era, I think, from the dress," I said. "She's very confused. Doesn't know she's dead. I haven't really figured out how to deal with her yet. I don't think she's dangerous."

"You don't *think*?" Jac repeated. She grabbed my arm.

"I want to hear everything that happened," she said, "but not . . ." she dropped her voice to a whisper, "in here. Let's go to the lake."

I let her lead me from the room. I'd had enough of Madame Serena for the time being, and I certainly didn't want to confuse her more by discussing the possible means of her death where she might overhear it. I thought there was a bathroom in the lobby, anyway.

I stole a last look into the room as I pulled the door closed. It was as still and quiet as a tomb.

Chapter 4

The lake really was spectacular. It was still fairly cool outside for late June, and the sun on my face felt glorious. Jac was practically bursting with excitement about the spirit in my room, and I have to say it made me feel great. Though she couldn't share in the actual experience of seeing dead people or trying to sort them out, Jac gobbled up everything I told her with an appetite she usually reserved for items in the cake family. And she gave good advice.

It had been Jac's idea to find out the name of the family who had once lived in the empty haunted house next door to mine over spring break. From there, we were able to use the computer to research what had happened to the family. It was like a detective game to her, and frankly, I was incredibly grateful for the company. It was easier taking on the spirit world when I knew that Jac always had my back.

"So spit it out, Voodoo Mama," Jac said.

I pointed to a little wooden bench perched in a sunny spot overlooking the lake.

"Let's go sit there," I said.

The bench was deliciously warm from the sunlight. A little frog perched half out of the water on a stone. A hawk was circling the rock face on the other side of the lake, and the breeze ruffled my hair. I could have sat there in perfect bliss forever.

"So?" Jac prompted, sitting next to me with her legs curled under her body.

"Okay, so I go into the room, and the second I turn around, she's there. Blam."

"Blam," Jac repeated.

"And she's dressed like Queen Victoria, so I'm figuring she goes pretty far back."

Jac nodded eagerly.

"I explain that I can see her, only when she starts talking, I realize she thinks that *she's* the one seeing a ghost. She called me 'spirit.'"

"She thought you were dead? That's kind of creepy," Jac said. Her grin indicated that in Jac's book, creepy was good.

"And she was talking about how we had a lot of work to do, because she'd been waiting a long time for me to show up. There was a fox, or something, that put her in danger.

And we're supposed to do something in a circle. In the room."

"Witchcraft," Jac murmured hopefully. "The fox was her animal familiar. Like in *The Golden Compass.*"

"I don't think so," I replied. "Anyway, it didn't seem like the right thing to do to just blurt out that she was dead. I'm not even sure she'd have believed me. She seemed to misunderstand everything I did try to tell her. I figured maybe I could do some poking around, and someone around here might help me find out who she was.

"I didn't tell her I was a medium. I just told her my name. Oh, I almost forgot — this is the most ridiculous part. She somehow decided I was some kind of Indian spirit guide, and she misunderstood me when I told her my name was Kat. So she thinks I'm this Native American astral entity called Simple Cat."

Jac threw her head back and howled with amusement. I felt a tiny bit irritated. I mean, yeah — it was funny. But maybe not *that* funny.

"Simple Cat," Jac said through her guffaws. "Oh, that's priceless, Voodoo Mama."

"Yeah, okay," I said. "Don't rupture your spleen or anything. But seriously. There must be a way to find out something about Madame Serena. Any ideas where I could start?"

Jac narrowed her eyes in thought. Then she sat up very straight. At first, I thought she'd gotten an idea. But she was staring very intently at the lake path behind me.

"No way," Jac whispered. "That looks like . . ."

She fell silent and I heard footsteps approaching. I was tactful enough not to turn around and gawk.

The footsteps slowed as they were right behind me.

"Hey! Jac, right? Cello genius, wassup!"

Jac's face was sheer pink. *Now* I turned around to gawk, and had to catch my breath.

The boy behind me had the face of a movie star, with jet black hair and eyes so blue they were practically hypnotic. My eyes were soon drawn to his hands, which were weirdly beautiful, like the hands of a gifted surgeon.

"Oh. Yeah, I mean, it's me," Jac stammered. "Hi, Colin. Wow. I mean, not wow, I just didn't realize . . . you know, yeah. That you were coming to this . . . thing. Right.

And this is my friend Kat. Kat, this is Colin —
soon to be the world's next reigning violin
virtuoso."

The movie star laughed, and brushed a
lock of hair out of his eyes. He wore jeans
and a faded purple T-shirt. He was slightly
built — slim and quite short. God, he didn't
need to be tall with a face like that. I made
some kind of noise that resembled "Hi."

"You missed the Junior Strings and
Woodwinds thing in May," Colin said,
coming around to stand in front of us. The
sun lit him from behind and made him
look like something Michelangelo should
have painted. "And you haven't posted on
the Classics Forum for a while. Revert to
lurking?"

Jac giggled strangely, and waved her
hand in front of her face. "Yeah, no, I just . . .
took myself out of the loop for a while."

Colin smiled, and my intestines quivered powerfully.

"Sounds like there's a story there," he said.

Jac nodded. Her smile didn't look like the regular Jac smile. She had clamped her lips closed over her teeth.

"What do you play, Kat?" he asked, turning his blue lamps of glory in my direction.

I play dead people, I thought.

But that was a bit of an overshare.

"I'm just along to keep Jac company," I said.

"Excellent," Colin said. My stomach did another little dance.

"Yes, I am," said my voice.

Brilliant. Future Rhodes Scholar.

"I was about to head over to the welcome reception," Colin said. "Were you gonna go?"

The question was obviously addressed

to Jac, and she nodded, the color of her face now having arrived at a solid brick red.

"Yeah, I was going to check it out," Jac lied.

"Cool. We can go together. I hate walking into those things alone. You coming, Kat?"

To the ends of the earth, Colin, if that's where you're going. But I snuck a sidelong glance at Jac. She was practically crippled by the blush, her eyes huge and her hands slightly trembling. The world's most gorgeous violin virtuoso had asked my best friend to go to a reception where I technically didn't belong. If there was a Best Friend's Handbook, I'm sure there was a whole chapter on what to do when the Cutest Boy Ever asks your friend to go somewhere. I'm betting the whole thing can be summed up as Three's. A. Crowd.

"Nah, I'm just going to hang here," I said.

"You guys go have fun talking Mozart, or whatever it is you do."

"Okay, great," Jac said, almost crushing my foot as she got up.

It would have been nice for her to make just a teensy argument, maybe pretend to want me to go along with them.

But another glance at the Face that Launched a Thousand Chicks and I swallowed my irritation and felt genuinely happy for Jac.

"I'll meet you in your room before dinner, okay?" she called.

I said, "Great." I probably could have said anything. Her ears had turned such an alarming shade of crimson I doubted they were working properly.

I snuck discreet glances at the happy couple making their way toward Mountain House. They actually looked good together.

Jac was really tiny, and Colin wasn't more than three or four inches taller than she was.

It was only when they were out of sight that I realized Jac had left me alone with my Madame Serena problem.

Chapter 5

Since I now had an unplanned block of time on my hands, I decided to follow the path around the lake. An old wooden footbridge arched over a gully and led up a steep staircase to the path on the far side of the lake. From there you could go in any number of different directions on marked trails. I took the one that was the steepest, and in half an hour I was atop an old fire tower, looking down at the spectacular lake and the massive building and gardens of Whispering Pines Mountain House.

I got a perfect cell signal up there, so I took the opportunity to call my mom.

"Well, it all sounds amazing, Kat," she said. "You guys should have a great time."

"I just wish you could see it," I told her truthfully. "I think you'd love it here."

"Take plenty of pictures for me," she said. "I'm going to have an entire new garden bed raked and cleared by the time you get back."

"That's great, Mom," I said. My mother did love her plants.

"Is something bothering you, Kat?" she asked.

"Why would you say that?" I asked innocently.

There was a slight pause.

"I don't know. Just a feeling. I thought maybe you had run into a visitor there, or something, and wanted to talk about it."

My mom sometimes called spirits "visitors." But she was a medium, not a mind-reader. How could she know about Madame Serena, or any other spirit here?

"No worries, Mom. I'm having a blast."

It wasn't exactly a lie. But ever since I had started seeing spirits, I had this stubborn inclination to want to deal with them myself, without asking Mom for help. I needed to figure things out in my own way.

"Well, give Jac a hug from me. And tell Mrs. Gray I said hello."

It's weird when your mother calls your friend's mother Mrs. So-and-so, but Jac's mom was super-formal. Did we even know her first name?

"I will, Mom. And I'll call again soon."

"Love you, sweetie. Bye."

After we hung up, I sat on a rock watching the world for a long time. I could see cars pulling up to the front entrance and families with enormous piles of luggage going inside. I felt a twinge of envy. Imagine being in a family where you could just head off to a place like this for a week or two. I'm betting it cost more to stay here for one night than my mother made in a week. But to some people, that was nothing at all. Chump change.

Mom and I had never had much money. When my dad dumped us to wallow in his midlife crisis, we were completely on our own. He never sent so much as a ten dollar bill in a birthday card. Not to this day. I guess my mom could have taken him to court, sued for child support. But she didn't. She said that money was just energy in another form, and that money from a negative source was nothing more than negative energy. And we got by. Sometimes more than got by.

There was money for what we needed, and occasionally some for something I wanted. It was usually enough. And I wouldn't trade my mom for anything in the world. But every once in a while, seeing a place like Whispering Pines and realizing where money could take a person, could take Jac's family, I felt a bit wistful.

When the sun went behind a large cloud, I suddenly felt chilly. I headed back down the path and over the bridge. I could hear music and laughter coming from a large room near the front of the building and wondered if it was Jac's reception. I smiled as I brought to mind a vision of the extraordinary shade of red Jac had turned in Colin's presence. I'm so glad I'm not a blusher. I may see dead people, but I stay the same color when I do.

When I reached my room, I was relieved

to find that Madame Serena wasn't there. I really didn't feel like being "Simple Cat, Guardian of the Sacred Portal of Transmigration" right then. I stretched out on my bed with a book, alternately reading and dozing. The last time, the sound of my stomach growling woke me up. I glanced at my watch — it was 6:30. Definitely dinnertime.

I guess Jac went back to her room, I thought. *Her mother's probably doing handsprings that she attended the reception. I should go rescue her.*

I brushed my hair and swished a little mouthwash over my teeth and gums, then left my room and knocked on the door across the hall.

"Jac? It's me, Kat. I'm starving."

The door opened. I was surprised and a little dismayed to find Jac's mother stand-

ing there. I assumed she'd be off hobnob-
bing with the other parents of prodigies.

"Oh, hi," I said. "I'm sorry. I was supposed to meet Jac right before dinner."

Mrs. Gray looked distracted and slightly
rumpled — very unusual for her. I noticed
she'd lost one of her earrings.

"Jackie?" she asked. "I thought she was
with you, Katherine. She said you were going to the lake."

"She was. We did," I said quickly. "But
she ran into this . . . there was another musician there that Jac knew. They went to the reception together."

Mrs. Gray's face brightened.

"Jackie went to the YNMC welcome
reception?"

I nodded. Mrs. Gray looked happy,
for once.

"Oh, I'm so pleased. Come in, Katherine. Have a seat. Who did you say she went with?"

Jac had never discussed her mother's position on boys. My suspicion was that, like most everything else that was interesting in the world, Mrs. Gray was against them.

"I'm really bad with names," I said. "It was a violin player, I think."

I felt a little strange telling the half truth — it stressed me out and made me feel dizzy. But I hadn't lied, really. I had just obscured the full details of the truth.

"I'm happy to hear that, Katherine. I'm glad you came with Jackie. She certainly had no intention of coming without you. I'm just going to pour myself a glass of Fiji water — would you like one?"

My mom and I loved to poke fun at people who drank designer water, but Mrs. Gray was being nice to me for a change, and I wanted to encourage her.

"Thank you, I'd love one," I said, reaching deep for my best manners.

She poured two glasses of water, then opened the ice bucket and sighed.

"Empty," she said. "I'll just go downstairs to get some more."

I nodded, and Mrs. Gray left the room.

My head was starting to feel even stranger, like I'd just gotten off one of those spinning rides at Playland. I gripped the arms of the chair I was sitting in and took a deep breath.

I was hit with a wave of sheer terror.

I gasped, pressing my hands over my chest. My heart was racing, and every inch of me was trembling. I'd dealt with being terrified before, but this was different. I felt more frightened than I'd ever felt in my life, but I had no idea why. As far as I could see, there was nothing in the room.

I really thought I might faint. My heart rate had practically doubled, and there was a rushing sound in my ears. Outside the bathroom, I paused and put my hand on the wall for support. I became aware of a sharp pain in the center of my chest, in the place where the ribs meet. Tears were streaming down my face from the pain and the terror. But I saw nothing! How could I know what to do if I couldn't see who or what I was dealing with?

Still leaning on the wall, I looked down at my feet. I was standing on something. Seeping into the wooden floor was a large pool of red paint.

No.

Blood.

Chapter 6

I yelled and jumped into the bathroom, slamming the door behind me. I crumpled to the floor and pulled my shoes off.

But there was no red sticky substance anywhere on them — not even the soles.

The silence was deafening.

But the feelings of terror, and the sharp pain in my chest, were subsiding. I took deep belly breaths, the way my mother's healer friend, Orin, had taught me. I heard the door to the room open.

"Katherine?"

"I'll be right out," I called.

I got to my feet a little shakily, and looked at my reflection. My face was pale. I flushed the toilet and ran the water in the sink to buy myself another minute to recover. I smoothed my hair back, pinched my cheeks to bring a little color into them, and put my shoes back on. Then I unlocked the door and went back into the room.

"Here you are," Mrs. Gray said, handing me a glass of water.

I gratefully took a long sip, secretly registering surprise that the water with the fancy name *did* taste better than tap water. I snuck a glance over my shoulder at the floor outside the bathroom. The planks looked just like the rest of the floor — polished and honey colored — no blood stain.

I was walking back to my chair when my toe connected with something. I leaned down and picked it up — it was Mrs. Gray's earring.

"I think this is yours," I said, handing it to her.

Her hands flew up to her ears.

"I didn't even know I'd lost it!" she exclaimed. "Thank you, Katherine. I'm feeling a little odd this afternoon; perhaps it was the drive. And the thermostat isn't working properly in this room — one minute, it's warm, and the next it's like an icebox."

I stared at the glass of water in my hand and chewed on my lip.

"And there's something . . . I don't know, a noise maybe? Like a very high-pitched electronic signal or something? Do you hear it?"

I shook my head.

"Maybe I'm imagining it. But something in this room is setting my teeth on edge."

The door opened, and Jac walked in.

"Kat! What are you doing in *here*?" Jac asked. "With *her*" was the unspoken remainder of her question.

"Looking for you. You said we'd meet before dinner."

It seemed weird to me that Jac hadn't even acknowledged her mother. I knew they really didn't get along and everything, but still. You say hello.

"Hello, Jackie. Katherine said you went to the welcome reception!"

"I stopped in for a minute," Jac replied, not looking at her mother. "Kat and I don't want to go to the fancy sit-down dining hall — can we just go by ourselves to the buffet thingy?"

Again, it seemed kind of rude for us to not eat with Jac's mom — I mean, she was footing the bill for the trip. But Mrs. Gray just nodded, and pressed a hand to her temple.

"That's fine, Jackie. I think I'm actually going to have a bit of a lie down — my head is really starting to ache."

"Bye," Jac said.

She already had the door open.

"I hope you feel better, Mrs. Gray," I said. "Can I get you anything before we go? An aspirin?"

She sat down on the edge of her bed.

"No thank you, Katherine. I just want to close my eyes for a while."

I closed the door quietly. Jac was waiting impatiently in the hall.

"What's with the sucking up?" she asked.

"I wasn't sucking up!" I retorted. "I was just being polite, which is more than I can say for you. Didn't you notice she kind of looked worn out?"

"I'm starting to think my mother has

you on the payroll," Jac said, striding down the hall toward the elevator.

"Don't be ridiculous."

The whole turn the conversation had taken was making me uncomfortable. I decided to change the subject.

"So? Are you going to tell me about this Colin guy?"

Jac came to a sudden stop and turned to me, her face shining.

"Oh, Kat, isn't he gorgeous?" she whispered.

I smiled.

"The boy is redonkulously good looking," I said. "I can't believe you've never mentioned him."

"Because he's barely ever spoken to me before!" she cried. "He goes to all the conferences and competitions in the area. He's, like, a celebrity at them. I most definitely knew who he was, but I had no idea he even knew I existed. When he called me Jac the cello genius, I thought I was going to pass out!"

"Yeah, I thought you might, too," I said, grinning. "So you went to this reception thing?"

Jac nodded excitedly. "Come on, I'm famished. I'll tell you all about it over dinner. I hope this place goes heavy on the desserts!"

I grinned and followed Jac to the elevator.

Still, I couldn't help but worry, just a little, about Mrs. Gray, alone with her sudden headache in that cold, eerie room.

Chapter 7

We ate in record time, me because I was starving and Jac because that's just the way she ate. Between heaping forkfuls of steaming lasagna, she detailed her experience with Colin at the welcome reception. There wasn't that much to tell, except that she and Colin stuck together for the entire reception, and that when they parted he told her he would "catch her later."

"Because you don't say 'catch you later' if it's something you don't want to happen, right?" Jac asked.

"I wouldn't think so," I replied.

"I mean, you could just say 'good-bye.' If you think about it, 'catch you later' could be like a statement of intent, you know? Like, I intend to catch you later."

"Could be," I said.

"Just in the way that, you know, he's letting me know that this could happen."

"Right, right," I said.

"Unless it just *is* something he says. Maybe 'catch you later' is just Colin's version of 'good-bye.'"

"Oh, I don't think so," I said.

"Really?" Jac cried. "Because the thing is, we did stick together for the entire reception. He never went off on his own."

This was the fourth time Jac had offered this detail to me. I looked around at the other tables. The buffet area was in a small room off the main lobby, which opened onto a wide screened-in porch overlooking the lake. We'd chosen to sit on the porch. About half the tables were occupied. Several of the diners were our age, but if they were fellow YNMC members, Jac didn't acknowledge them.

"Right, I know," I said.

"If you think about it, seriously, if he was just being polite by asking if I wanted to go to the reception, it'd be the easiest thing in the world to just split off once we got there. Don't you think? I mean, nobody would think anything of that, or get their feelings hurt. Right? But he didn't, Kat. Am I wrong to think that that's significant? Then he makes this comment about catching me later, and did I mention that he looked —"

"— you right in the eye and smiled when he said it? Yeah," I said. I had a square of lasagna left on my plate, and I began to stab my fork into it repeatedly.

"Because if it was just that comment, okay. Maybe it wouldn't mean anything. But the thing is, Kat, he stuck right by my side for the entire reception. Every single minute of it!"

Stab. Stab. Stab.

"Oh my god, I'm sorry," Jac said suddenly.

I looked up at her expectantly.

"I'm going on and on about this like some cheerleader groupie," Jac said. "I'm boring you silly trying to hyperanalyze everything that happened. I'm guessing you're pretending that lasagna you're mutilating is me."

I laughed, relieved that Jac herself had noticed how irritating the conversation had grown.

"It's okay," I said, putting down my fork. "I mean, yeah, I was getting a tiny bit tired of it. But at the same time, I understand. The guy looked totally obsession-worthy to me."

"We were going to figure out how to track down Madame Serena's story," Jac said.

Yay. She had remembered my problem after all.

"Right! There doesn't seem to be any such thing as computer access here — that's the thing. So we can't do the usual thing of searching archived newspaper articles."

"Maybe you could call your mom and ask her to do a search on her computer?" Jac said.

"I don't know. I really don't want to get my mom involved. Then I'll be, like, expected to keep her in the loop. We're supposed to be on vacation, right?"

"Absolutely," Jac declared.

"And the thing is, Jac, it isn't just Madame Serena. There's something else, something really bad, that I have to tell —"

"Oh my god, there he is!" Jac hissed, grabbing my arm.

I looked in the direction she was looking.

Colin was standing in the buffet room with another guy. He seemed to be filling a large travel mug with soda from the dispenser. Maybe he felt our eyes on him. He glanced in our direction, and his face brightened when he saw Jac. He waved and started walking over.

"Oh my god, he waved," Jac whispered. "Kat, he's *walking over here!*"

Thank you, yes. My eyeball-to-brain connection is working just fine.

Jac was dabbing furiously at her lips with a napkin, and I suspect she was thanking her lucky stars her plate wasn't heaped high with dessert items — if only because she had never stopped talking long enough to go load up.

"Hey, Jac, hey, Kat, wassup?" Colin asked as he reached our table.

In spite of everything, I couldn't help but be flattered the guy had remembered my name. Dead people followed me around like I was the Pied Piper of Tomb-lin, but living boys didn't often take much notice of me.

"Hey, Colin," Jac said. Her voice sounded higher than usual, and I resisted the impulse to kick her under the table.

"Austin and I are going to make the hike up to Sunset Ridge with Cleo — she's the clarinet player from Cape Cod? Figured we'd try to rustle up another couple musicians to come along. I mean, you're welcome, too, Kat."

"Honorary musician," I said, pointing to myself.

Colin laughed, and I swear I felt my appendix do a 360.

"Honorary musician, yeah. That's good."

Whunk.

I shot Jac a look and rubbed my leg. What was up with that? Jac had just kicked *me* under the table. She looked at me quickly, then looked away.

Jac didn't want me to go. She'd never say it, I knew. But she felt it. Jac wanted to go hike up to Sunset Ridge with Austin and the clarinet player from Cape Cod, and she didn't want me along to sidetrack Colin with my witty quips.

Or whatever.

"I've already hiked up to the fire tower today," I said. "My hamstrings are killing me. You guys go ahead. I'll tell your mom where you went, Jac."

"Are you sure? Okay," Jac said.

"Cool," said Colin. "I've got to catch up with Austin. Let's meet at the trailhead over by the boat launch in ten minutes, okay? The one near where you guys were sitting today."

"Definitely," Jac said. "I'll definitely be there."

"Excellent. Catch you later, Kat."

I stifled a smile as Colin walked away. Jac didn't seem as interested in analyzing the phrase "catch you later" when it was addressed to me.

"Oh my god, I'm so sorry," Jac said, when Colin was out of earshot. "Is it okay? I mean he kind of put me on the spot, just appearing and asking me out like that. I don't have to go. I could change my mind, you know."

It didn't seem like "rustling up another couple musicians" was the same thing as asking someone out, but I bit my lip. I was being selfish, begrudging Jac her hike with Dream Boy. And I was big enough to admit, if only to myself, that I was a little bit jealous of my best friend at the moment.

"No worries," I said. "Of course you're going, Jac. You'd be crazy not to."

"I know, right?" Jac said, in something dangerously close to a squeal. "You're the best, Kat. I promise to tell you every single detail."

Now, I just didn't have that kind of time.

Before I had even realized the conversation was over, Jac was on her feet and through the door, leaving me to bus her plate.

"Catch you later," I murmured.

I really hoped this was not an indication of how the next five days were going to be. But I told myself to be happy for Jac. Other than me, Jac didn't have any friends at school (which was fine, because I didn't have any other friends, either). She had a tough situation at home with her mother, who was pretty critical of her and who'd spent her whole life trying to mold Jac into a world-class musician. And her dad seemed to fly off to California on business at the drop of a hat. In short, Jac just didn't have all that many things going right in her life.

What kind of friend was I not to be psyched that Dream Boy was paying her some attention? When the conference was over, everything would go back to being not so right. As far as I was concerned, Jac could go to the moon with Colin. She deserved to be happy.

I dumped our leftover food and left the plates in the pick-up cart. It was only 7:45, way too early to think about curling up in bed with a book. I decided to explore some of the main floor of the Whispering Pines Mountain House.

The building was a funny patchwork of huge rooms, like the formal dining room and the rambling sitting room, with corridors that stretched out in odd directions, dotted with doors leading to little side rooms. I wandered around, poking into rooms as I came across them. Many of them were just small sitting rooms with bookshelves full of dusty old volumes.

One of the rooms had been made into a little nature center, with photographs of local wildlife, and a journal where guests could record what animals they saw, and where. I skimmed through it and was surprised to see that in addition to snakes, owls, and otters, the occasional black bear was spotted on the mountain. One guest with suspiciously childlike writing claimed to have seen the Abominable Snowman by the tennis courts just after breakfast.

Several doors down from the nature center I found a room that seemed to be devoted to the history of Whispering Pines. The walls were covered with old photographs, some of them old enough that the vehicles pictured were horse-drawn buggies. Other than the size of the Mountain House itself, which seemed to have quadrupled in the last century, the lake and the mountainside seemed remarkably untouched by time. I found a pamphlet with a brief history of Whispering Pines, and I curled up on the couch and began to read it.

It was warm in the room, and the more I read, the drowsier I felt. I closed my eyes for a moment, savoring the heat and deliberating whether I should actually let myself nod off. Then suddenly I was wide awake.

And I knew without a doubt I was no longer alone in the room.

Chapter 8

I opened my eyes to find I was being observed by a guy wearing a Whispering Pines employee name tag. Definitely not dead. He looked about the same age as me. Not to be mean, but his looks were . . . less than remarkable. He was on the short side, with a slightly squashed-down nose, reddish brown hair cut too short, and gray-blue eyes set a little too closely together. In fact, he reminded me of the Evolution of Man poster from the science classroom at school. His face was wide and flat and his forehead and brow were heavy. Kind of like a Cro-Magnon guy. Basically, he was the anti-Colin.

"Oh — you're awake. I'm sorry," said Cro-Magnon Boy, rubbing his hands together nervously.

Why was he sorry that I was awake? Maybe he thought I was as uncute as I thought he was.

"I was reading," I said, a little defensively. "It's hot. The room, I mean. Not the . . . thing I'm reading."

"I keep telling them these rooms need better circulation," Cro-Magnon Boy said, taking a few steps toward me. "Hey — is that the Mountain House history?"

I nodded. I wasn't sure how I felt about encouraging the conversation to continue. Cro-Magnon interaction hadn't been on my wish list for this vacation, or ever.

"Yeah," I said. "I was just flipping through

it. The pictures from back in the 1800s are amazing. I sort of like it — knowing that this place has been around so long. There's got to be tons of cool stories and stuff."

Cro-Magnon Boy's face lit up. Clearly, I'd said something very right.

"My great-great-great-great-grandfather built this place," he said.

"Great. I mean, seriously?"

CMB pointed at the couch I was sitting on. "Mind if I sit?"

"Sure," I said.

I hoped I hadn't made a mistake. Telling CMB he could sit down was kind of a commitment.

"And yes, seriously. My great-great-great-great-grandparents were Thaddeus and Clementine Kenyon. Thaddeus built this hotel in 1841, and the Kenyon family has been running it ever since. Whispering Pines Mountain House is the oldest continuously operating hotel in the country, and the only one that has never changed hands over the course of one and a half centuries."

CMB talked like a brochure. But I have to say, I was kind of impressed.

"I'm Kat Roberts," I said. "So you must be, like, a hotel heir or something."

Ted burst out laughing. His flattish features looked much nicer when he smiled, and his gray-blue eyes glittered.

"Not exactly," he said. "There are quite a few direct Kenyon descendants. I'm one of about thirty. My dad and two of my uncles run the place, which their dad did before them for forty years. Between their kids and their cousins' kids, there's always a good supply of Kenyons working the Mountain House on summers and holidays."

"It's nice of you to chip in," I said.

"Oh, I actually look forward to it. One day, after college I guess, I'm going to work here full time. Maybe even run the place. I practically grew up at the Mountain House. That's why I dorked out when I saw you were reading the history pamphlet, which my mom wrote, by the way. I'm going to write a book about it — the whole Mountain House story."

"Really?" I asked, impressed for the second time in less than five minutes by Cro-Magnon Boy. The guy had goals.

Ted was doing the nervous hand-rubbing thing again. He was doing it with his feet too — grinding the toe of his left Reebok over the laces of his right Reebok.

"So you probably know a whole lot about the Mountain House in the 1800s," I said.

"Are you kidding? I know it all!" Ted exclaimed. "Okay. That didn't come out the way I meant it to. But yeah, my grandfather used to tell stories for days at a time."

"Okay," I began, "this might sound weird. But does the name Madame Serena mean anything to you?"

Ted laughed again, transforming his face from Cro-Magnon to not all that bad.

"You've been doing your homework!" he exclaimed, pleased. "Yeah, wow. Let me think a sec."

He propped his feet up on the table, still clutching his hands together like they might do something nutty if he released them.

"Well for starters, Madame Serena came to the Mountain House during the Spiritualist movement. Do you know much about the Spiritualists?"

I didn't know what to say about that. I

considered myself somewhat of an expert on anything that had the word *spirit* in it, but I'd never heard of Spiritualists. So I curled my feet under me, got comfortable, and stared at him wide-eyed. My plan worked, because he took a deep breath and kept talking without waiting for me to answer.

"The Spiritualist movement started up around the same time the Mountain House was built. If memory serves, people linked the beginning of the movement to the Foxes."

Madame Serena had said something about a fox!

"Foxes from where?" I asked.

"I think there were two or three of them," Ted said. "The Fox sisters. Margaret was the most famous. Anyway, to totally oversimplify things, the idea behind the movement was the belief that the spirits of dead people could be contacted by mediums."

I didn't mean for it to happen, but my mouth dropped wide open.

"No, no —" he said, putting his hand out in the universal "stop" position. "Don't even say it. I'm not saying I believe in all that stuff. I'm a historian, not a nut job. I'm just telling you what *they* believed."

I couldn't think of a thing to say. Part of me wanted to punch Ted Kenyon in his already squashed-down nose, but part of me wanted to hear more of the story.

"The story goes that the Fox sisters made contact with the ghost of a murdered peddler in their farmhouse, around 1848 or '49, I think. They said the peddler told them he had been murdered by the farmer who had lived there, and his things were stolen and his body buried in the cellar. And the thing was, they didn't just do it once. They could establish contact at any time, and when they asked this spirit to make a knocking sound, it did. Hundreds of people came and witnessed it. Before too long, people all over the country were hiring mediums and having séances. And the Spiritualists were born. The whole thing was utterly ridiculous," he added, shaking his head.

I thought about punching his nose again.

"Well, if hundreds of people heard it, why are the Spiritualists ridiculous?" I asked, trying to sound casual, like I didn't care much one way or the other what the answer was.

"The Fox sisters got really famous, and suddenly everybody wanted to be a 'medium.' And of course there was an unlimited supply of kooks willing to pay good money to supposedly contact their dead loved ones. It was the thing to do, in those days. It was a fad, a craze. Like . . . disco."

DISCO?

"It was nothing more than a business venture, a scam. And a lot of these so-called mediums started making names for themselves. Then they could really charge top dollar."

So-called mediums?

"And they'd develop followings, and host these gatherings called salons where they'd have tea and cakes, and then hold séances. It became the Victorian version of the Oprah book club.

"Anyway, one of these mediums lived here at the Mountain House for about a year — she had her own room where she conducted her so-called séances. She was apparently not even very good at *faking* being a medium. Quite the old bat, from what I've read. And, as you might have guessed by now, she called herself Madame Serena."

Then he gave me this look and he chuckled and shook his head. Like he just *assumed* that I agreed with him — that *any* sane human being would automatically and without question agree that a person styling themselves as a so-called medium was a faker, an old bat. Insane. A laughingstock. And that anyone stupid enough to believe in mediums was a nut job.

I didn't know I was going to say it. I just saw red.

"Who do you think you are?" I demanded, sitting up very straight and scowling. Ted drew back, like I had in fact already punched his silly misshapen nose and was winding up for a second go.

"I'm sorry?" he asked. He looked genuinely distressed.

"I just don't know how you can sit there and mock an entire group of people, millions of people actually, who either believe they can communicate with the dead, or believe that someone else can. I mean, where do you get off making a decision like that?"

Ted stared at me, his mouth open.

"I mean, did I miss some sort of global memo that was issued stating *Hey, we can cross off the old life-after-death thing from our list of ancient questions, because Ted of the Whispering Pines Mountain House has just announced that the whole thing is —* how'd you put it — *utterly ridiculous?*"

Ted's mouth was opening and closing a little, like he was trying to talk. He looked like an anxious fish.

"I just want to know who you think you

are," I repeated, my voice getting louder than I meant it to. But hey, I was on a roll.

"Who are *you*, Ted Kennedy, to make —"

"Ted Kenyon," he whispered.

"What?" I spluttered.

"I'm not Ted Kennedy, I'm Ted Kenyon —" he said, in a voice barely above a whisper.

"Who are *you*, Ted *Kenyon*, to make this proclamation to the world?"

There was a pause long enough for him to assume this wasn't a rhetorical question.

"Nobody," he said quietly. His face was beet red.

"Okay, then!"

I got to my feet.

To be honest, I was actually kind of embarrassed at this point. I'd meant to call Ted out on his categorical dismissal of my entire life, but I had never intended to make a scene. But I *had* made a scene, so I needed to come up with a Big Finish and get the heck out of there.

"Then you might want to keep your assumptions to yourself," I said. "And the next time you decide to flat out dismiss a belief system held by millions of people, the next time you get all holier-than-thou and condescending about an idea that's been around since the dawn of man, maybe you'll give it a second thought!"

Then I stomped out of the room as self-righteously as I could. When I got to the hallway I started to sprint, and I didn't slow down until I got to the elevator, which was mercifully there and waiting. The last thing I needed was for Cro-Magnon Boy to come running after me.

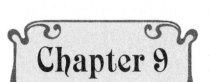

Chapter 9

By the time I'd reached the hallway leading to room 505, I was feeling ridiculous. The world was full of people like Ted. People who mocked belief in the supernatural. For years, I'd witnessed this happening to my mom — someone would find out she was a medium and act like they had this Free Mockery card.

Before we moved, I had a friend in the third grade who was really fat. I never really thought about her size one way or another — she was just Tessa. But sometimes the kids in class would rag on her and call her names, and nobody did anything about it.

One day I asked Tessa why she accepted this treatment without fighting back. She told me what her mom had told her — that some people in the world felt entitled to insult fat people, that no matter how messed up someone was they could always console themselves by feeling superior to a person who was overweight. And that she had learned to accept it, rather than waiting for the world to change. Because inside, she knew her own worth.

I never got the impression Tessa felt like it was okay for kids to rag on her. Just that they did, that they probably always would, and that she wasn't going to let it get to her. Now I was starting to understand what a difficult thing that must have been for her.

To much of the world, my mother and I would always be a source of amusement, at best, and contempt, at worst. I thought of Brooklyn Bigelow back at school — first lady-in-waiting to the celestial entity of popularity: Shoshanna. When Brooklyn found out my mother was a medium, she practically bubbled over with venom. She truly thought she'd found a nugget of hidden information so scandalous it would drive us from town in disgrace.

Not everybody was as bad as Brooklyn. But there were too few Jacs in the world. Be that as it may, I couldn't go ballistic every time some dillweed like Ted sounded off about people like my mom and me.

Better luck next time.

By the time I unlocked my room, all I wanted was to go to bed and let sleep blot out the events of the evening. I opened the door and hurried inside, then stopped.

Madame Serena was sitting on my bed.

Her eyes were closed, and her lips were moving. She was wearing some kind of turban, with a glittering pin fastened in its center. Her face looked tinted by orange — as if she were illuminated by a phantom candle. I couldn't make out what she was chanting. I stood there and waited for her to finish, hoping it wouldn't take too long.

I knew enough now to guess that Madame Serena had conducted séances in my room, and that she believed herself to be conducting one now. It was a start.

I sat down on the bed next to her.

She mumbled a bit more, then I was able to pick out her words.

"Return to me, Simple Cat."

"I'm right here," I said quietly, so as not to disrupt the mood.

Madame Serena did not open her eyes.

"I await you," she intoned. "I command —"

"Hello!" I barked.

Madame Serena shrieked and jumped half a foot in the air. If she'd been a living person of that size, I would have been propelled across the room when she landed back on the mattress. But her phantom bulk had no effect, though her turban was now slightly askew on her head. I thought it looked kind of sporty that way.

"Oh!" Madame Serena exclaimed, pressing her hand to her chest. Sitting so close to her, I noticed the enormous rings she wore, dwarfing even her ample-sized fingers.

"Simple Cat," Madame Serena said. "You have returned."

"Just Kat," I said. "You can call me just Kat, okay?"

"Oh Simple Cat," Madame Serena said, talking right through me. "I welcome you to the world of the living. There are humans on this side of the veil that are most eager to connect with their loved ones."

I sighed, and arranged myself with legs crossed under me, facing Madame Serena on the bed.

"About the world of the living . . . that's something I need to talk to you about," I said carefully. "The . . . side of the veil that you're on, and all that."

"Yes!" Madame Serena said excitedly. "You are urgently needed here, Simple Cat. I feel most obliged to begin with the Colonel's wife. She has been to see me each week for almost a year now, hoping to contact her Loretta. Her situation is most desperate.

"The loss of Loretta almost killed the poor woman, and I'm afraid her health is still dangerously delicate. I have promised to reunite her with Loretta, and I fear that my failure to do so may prove catastrophic to her heart. Do you see Loretta, Simple Cat? Has she joined you there?"

"Just Kat," I said, very slowly and deliberately.

Madame Serena looked agitated.

"Simple and Just Cat, of course. Do you see Loretta? Is she nearby?"

Right. I better drop my attempts to correct my name before I ended up Simple and Just and Wise and Slightly Fat in the Butt Cat, or worse. As for Loretta, she was not nearby. The only spirit in the room was Madame Serena, which was lucky for me. Madame Serena was just about all I could take at the moment.

"Um, about this . . . Colonel's wife?" I asked.

Madame Serena nodded gravely.

"Well, I don't, uh . . . where exactly is she, Madame Serena?"

The medium sighed deeply, and looked on the point of tears.

"It's most vexing," she told me. "Now that you have come, Simple and Just Cat, now that I have finally raised a Guardian of the Sacred Portal of Transmigration after trying for so many months, I'm afraid the Colonel's wife has given up on me."

"Given up on you?" I asked.

Madame Serena nodded again.

"I can only assume this is the case. The Colonel's wife, as I said, has kept our appointment each week for almost one full year. She travels by coach from Rochester to the Mountain House — so it is no small trip for her. But she has not arrived today. I fear, Simple and Just Cat, that she has given up trying to see her Loretta on the very day you have come across the veil to assist her!"

"I . . . I'm sorry about that," I said. "And let's just stick with Simple Cat, okay?"

I was really trying to buy time, because it was all very confusing. The Colonel's wife, whoever she was, would of course be long dead by now. So technically, she was on Madame Serena's side of the veil, as she put it. With Loretta. Why both of them couldn't simply let Madame Serena know this was confusing.

The key had to be that Madame Serena didn't know *she* was dead. Presumably both the Colonel's wife and Loretta *did* know they were dead, and had moved on to wherever they were supposed to be, while Madame

Serena was still hanging around room 505 conducting her séances.

Or her séance.

Just one séance. A séance she was now re-living. Probably the last one. Madame Serena said the Colonel's wife came every week for almost a year, so that would make around fifty séances where she'd attempted to contact the spirit of Loretta. And failed. And finally, say on week fifty-one, the poor Colonel's wife finally gave up and didn't come back. This was the loop in time in which Madame Serena was stuck.

But why couldn't Madame Serena contact this Loretta? Given fifty tries, Madame Serena ought to have been able to get some sort of result. Unless Ted had been right about one thing.

Maybe Madame Serena was a fake.

"Loretta," Madame Serena was calling in a singsong voice. "Loretta — come to the Simple Cat. She will guide you to the Colonel's wife, who loves you deeply and mourns your passing with a cavernous anguish of grief!"

Madame Serena's voice trembled. She seemed to be moving herself to tears with her own words.

"Perhaps this isn't the right time to focus on Loretta," I suggested.

Madame Serena gave a little sob, and retrieved a handkerchief from the sleeve of her gown.

"Poor, dear Loretta," she said. "The Colonel's wife said she was not but two years old when she passed."

That was sad.

"Madame Serena," I said. "We need to

talk about something else before we can help the Colonel's wife find Loretta."

She looked at me, wide-eyed and tearful. Her turban was drooping over one eyebrow.

"What is it, Simple Cat?" Madame Serena asked, in a voice barely above a whisper. Like maybe she suspected it wasn't necessarily good news.

Someone banged on my door.

Finally, Jac!

"Madame Serena, I need to —" I stopped midsentence.

She had gone.

It was just as well. I needed to get my head around who was where in the afterlife, and how to best sort them all out. I opened the door with an expectant smile.

"Mrs. Gray!" I said, surprised.

"I'm sorry to bother you, Katherine,"

she said. "But is Jackie in here? It's almost nine o'clock, and she hasn't been back to our room."

I stifled a cry of dismay.

"I was supposed to tell you! I'm so sorry, Mrs. Gray. Jac went for a walk with some of the musicians, and I told her I'd let you know. It's my fault — I completely forgot!"

Mrs. Gray nodded and sighed.

"No, it's quite all right Katherine, thank you. I'm just glad to know where she is. I'm afraid I missed dinner and the Parents of Protégés meeting — my head ached so dreadfully I just couldn't leave my room. Perhaps I'm coming down with something."

I studied Mrs. Gray's face in the dim light. She did look a bit odd — not the polished, perfect face I was accustomed to.

"Do you want me to run downstairs and see if I can rustle you up something to eat?" I asked.

She gave me a wan smile.

"Thanks, Katherine. That's very kind of you, but I'm really not hungry. I'll just get comfortable with a good book and wait for Jackie to come back."

Somehow I doubted that Jac was going to be too chatty with her mother when she returned. She had seemed awfully anti-mother when I left her. I felt a flash of irritation at my best friend. I knew she wanted to sleep in my room, but I suddenly resolved to lock my door, and leave a note that I'd gone to sleep. For tonight, at least, let Jac be stuck in her mom's room. Maybe she'd relent and let her mom know she'd been hanging out with a boy.

I normally didn't go to bed this early, but suddenly curling up under the covers was all I wanted to do. It would be a peaceful and refreshing night.

I couldn't have been more wrong.

Chapter 10

I was standing in the hallway outside my room. I had no idea what time it was, or even how I'd gotten out of my room. I must have been sleepwalking. From the absolute lack of sound and light I guessed it must be around three in the morning.

What on earth am I doing here? I wondered. There certainly didn't seem to be any reason that I'd come into the hallway. I had never been a sleepwalker. I decided to go back into my room immediately, and get into bed again, hoping this was a onetime deal.

But I couldn't move.

My feet were rooted to the floor, and I couldn't even wiggle my fingers. A feeling of panicked doom began to overtake me.

I was facing the door to room 504, where Jac and her mom were sleeping. I opened my mouth to call out to Jac. Yeah, it'd be embarrassing to have the two of them come out and find me there. But I needed help, and right now I didn't care how it looked.

I could barely make a tiny exhaling sound. I couldn't even whisper Jac's name. No power to move, no power to speak. And the feeling of doom kept growing. My eyes were stuck on the door to room 504.

It flew open with a bang.

Inside the room, it was pitch black. Actually, it was even darker than that.

Back at school, when Jac and I were trying to contact the spirit of Suzanne Bennis, we'd gone to the school library at dawn to have a séance. I saw something there that day — something I tried not to think about. A thing that was neither human nor spirit. It was more of a . . . presence. A presence that hung in an inky black cloud that was not so much a dark shape, but the absolute absence of light. A malevolent black hole.

I was seeing the same shape now, in the room before me. The room where my best friend and her mother were sleeping.

I had to wake them!

The more I tried to scream and the harder I attempted to move forward, the more frozen I became. I felt as if my entire body was turning to ice, and in fact I could see a cloud of vapor forming in front of my mouth every time I breathed out. The large window at the end of the hallway was open, but there was no way, even on a cool night in June, that it was anywhere near freezing outside. I struggled to get even an inch closer to the room, determined to get through that door no matter what it took.

Until the black cloud inside the room began to move toward me.

I could feel the thing more clearly than I could see it. Its closeness made me shake uncontrollably and feel physically sick. It bore no resemblance to anything I'd sensed from human spirits. But it seemed to have intelligence. Or at least desire. Because every cell in my body sensed that this thing wanted to cause harm — to me or any human it could reach. And it was still moving closer.

It wasn't until the black cloud was almost on top of me that I remembered the energy blocks that Orin had taught me. I envisioned a golden bubble of light springing up around me like a force field. I sent a call for protection to the grid of energy Orin called the Divine Matrix. The darkness was still advancing, but as it reached me I could feel resistance. The cloud was not swallowing me up like I suspected it meant to.

It was pushing against me. But for the first time, I felt like I was able to push back.

I am protected, I thought, as forcefully as possible. *You cannot touch me.*

But it was strong. It was so incredibly powerful. Though it couldn't seem to penetrate the bubble of energy I'd created, it moved against me so hard I felt my feet slipping and sliding on the floor. There didn't seem to be anything I could do to get rid of it, though being so near the black cloud made me frantic — like I was covered with spiders or cockroaches. The sensation was unbearable.

It pushed me harder and harder. Not

toward my room, and not back into room 504. The cloud was pushing me down the hall. Fast. Right toward the huge window that stood open and inviting like a magic door into the night.

I suddenly realized what the black cloud was trying to do.

"No!" I yelled, finding my voice. "Let me go!"

My command had no effect. I felt something hard against my leg, and looked down to see the window ledge pressing into my thigh.

I would not let it. I could not let the black cloud push me out that window.

But suddenly there was nothing under my feet. I felt the hard surface of the window ledge brush beneath me, and I reached out and grabbed either side of the window frame with both hands. I dug my nails into the wood as tightly as I could. For a minute, I thought I might be okay.

Then something slammed into my back like a giant fist, and I was pushed over the windowsill, and my mind only had time to register the fresh cool air, a glimpse of a spectacular night sky, and a sickening whoosh as the ground rushed five stories to collide with my body.

Chapter 11

When my body hit, the surface was impossibly soft and flexible. I opened my eyes, gasping for breath, and looked up at the ceiling of my room. I had kicked the covers down into a ball by my feet. The digital clock on the bedside table said 3:37.

I burst into tears.

To say that I'd had a bad dream was like calling the *Titanic* a bad boat trip. Clearly, I was back in bed and not splattered on the Mountain House lawn, but whatever had gone on was much more than a nightmare.

I didn't think I'd ever get back to sleep, and I actually didn't want to, for fear the whole thing might start up again. But the last time I remembered looking at the clock it was 4:15, and when I opened my eyes again the room was bright with sunlight.

The rays of sun streaming through the window were more comforting than I could possibly explain. I lay in bed like a statue, savoring the warmth and light on my face. I felt like I could stay that way all day, but the peaceful moment was interrupted by a loud knock on my door.

"Yeah?" I called.

"It's almost eleven o'clock. What are you doing?"

I didn't want to get up and open the door. I'd locked it before going to sleep, but maybe when I was sleepwalking . . . but no. There had been no sleepwalking. I'd awakened in my own bed, proof it had been a dream. Wasn't it?

The door opened and Jac marched in, looking none too pleased with me. She didn't give me time to wonder about the door being unlocked after all; she just started right in on me.

"Thank you so much," Jac said, standing with her arms folded over her chest and looking decidedly unthankful.

"Wha — ?" That was all I could muster. I wanted to stay in bed with the sun on my face, not join the world, which at this moment was represented by Jac, and a cranky one at that.

"No, really, I'm so *incredibly* grateful."

"Um . . . you're welcome?"

I hoped Jac might be serious, and not sarcastic. She could be referring to the graceful way in which I'd allowed her to head off with Dream Boy, leaving me all by myself. But Jac's expression was now unmistakable — she was glowering at me. Not a happy camper.

"Ugh, what is your *problem*," Jac cried, stamping one tiny foot on the floor. "I come back upstairs last night and your door is locked and there's this Post-it telling me you've gone to sleep and I have to go spend the night with my mother! I mean seriously, Kat — what is wrong with you?"

I pulled the covers up to my chin, wanting to hide under them.

"Nothing," I said. "It's what the note said. I got tired. I went to bed."

And locked the door, or so I thought.

"This week was supposed to be you and me," Jac said, her arms still folded over her chest. "Do you honestly think I came to this conference to have a slumber party with *my mother?* We're supposed to be hanging out, Kat! You totally blew me off!"

Abandoning the comfort of the covers, I sat up in bed.

"Oh really?" I cried. "Is that your version of who blew off whom, Jac? You dumped me by the lake for Dream Boy, then you dumped me at dinner for Dream Boy, then you get all torqued out because when you finally come looking for me I'm sleeping?"

Jac opened her mouth and took a deep breath, then stopped and shut her mouth. She stood over me scowling, but I knew Jac's expression. This particular scowl indicated thought, not anger.

"You said it ... I mean, it was only because ..."

Jac paused, and sat down on the edge of the bed.

"I mean," she continued more quietly, "I

thought you said it was okay for me to go with Colin."

Her green eyes filled with tears and she looked away to hide the fact.

"It *was* okay," I said. "I was psyched for you, Jac. I still am. But I ended up kind of having a boring night, with a little Cro-Magnon drama thrown in, and I don't think you should have all this attitude just because I went to bed early."

She turned her face toward me, the tears gone.

"You're right, Kat. Totally right. I'm just in a bad mood because I had to spend the night sharing a bed with *her.* I'm sorry."

I looked at her face carefully. There were no dark circles under *her* eyes.

"It's okay. Yeah, um, how'd you sleep?"

"How did I sleep?" Jac asked.

I nodded.

"Fine, I guess," she said. "In spite of the fact that I had to share a bed with my mother."

"It's a king-sized bed," I pointed out. "The bed in there is, like, bigger than my bathroom at home. It's bigger than our whole car!"

"It wasn't big enough," Jac said ruefully. "She kept tossing and turning all night. Muttering things, or something."

"She did? But you slept okay?" I repeated.

"God, yes, I slept fine. Are we on hidden camera or something?" Jac asked.

You have no idea, I thought.

"Did something happen last night?" Jac said, her eyes suddenly gleaming. "Tell me!"

But I wasn't ready to talk about that.

"Like I said, I was wiped out and I went to sleep. End of story."

Jac grabbed one of my pillows, and

stretched out on her back propping herself up on one of the bedposts.

"Then what did you mean by Cro-Magnon drama?" she demanded. "Something did so happen, and I want to know what."

I was relieved to have the chance to talk about something other than room 504.

"Ugh, I went to one of the sitting rooms last night and I ended up meeting this guy," I began.

"What?" Jac shrieked.

"This *horrible* guy. He works here — actually, he's like a Whispering Pines brat — his family owns the place."

Jac waggled her eyebrows, but I shook my head.

"No, seriously, I've seen better looking hobbits," I said. "It's not like that. This was no Colin, Maestra. I was sitting there reading this pamphlet about the history of the

Mountain House, because I still needed to find out stuff about Madame Serena. He came in, and started talking to me, and he knew who Madame Serena was."

Jac sat up.

"No way!" she exclaimed. "So, who was she?"

"A so-called medium," I told her.

"So-called . . . what?"

"Yeah," I said. "His words. My reaction exactly. He's telling me basically that Madame Serena lived here in the late 1800s, and I guess she had clients that came to her trying to contact their departed relatives. But he totally mocked the whole concept, you know, and he's looking at me and laughing like 'How pathetic for anyone to claim to be a so-called medium . . .' and anyway, I lost my temper and stormed out. There you have it — my Cro-Magnon drama in a nutshell."

"Oh, I wish I'd been there," Jac said. "I would have taught him a lesson."

"Well," I said a little sheepishly, "I think he got the message. I laid into him pretty thick."

"Good!" Jac declared. "What a jerk. He sounds like the male version of Brooklyn Bigelow."

I laughed.

"I'm starving," Jac announced suddenly.

"You're always starving."

"I'm especially starving at this moment," she insisted.

I swung my legs over the side of the bed, reluctantly leaving the sunlight.

"Okay, okay," I said. "Don't have an episode. Let me get dressed and brush my teeth and we'll go down to get something to eat."

"Hurry," Jac commanded, and I rolled my eyes.

But as I walked past her toward the bathroom, she reached out and grabbed my arm.

"Hey, Voodoo Mama," she said softly. "I really am sorry about blowing you off."

"It's okay," I said.

"It isn't okay," Jac insisted. "You're my best friend. This is our week to hang out together. Because of me, we've started off badly."

"We've started off *fine,* " I said. "Now let go of me so I can go pee."

Jac obeyed, and installed herself in the sunny spot on the bed while I went into the bathroom.

I brushed my teeth and hair, threw on some jeans and a long-sleeved shirt, shoved my feet into my sandals, and I was ready to roll.

"Finally," Jac said theatrically. "I thought I was going to waste away."

I swatted her on the arm.

"I'm sure you have a Twinkie reserve in your suitcase that you haven't told me about," I said, grabbing the key to the room.

"Why, do you want one?" Jac asked, grinning.

"No thanks," I said, as we walked into the hallway. "You know I'm more of an oatmeal and toast girl."

"Don't sell yourself short," Jac said, shifting from one foot to the other as I fiddled with the key. After two tries, the lock clicked and I slid the key out and put it in my pocket.

Jac started down the hallway in the direction of the elevator. I stood where I was, my eyes on the door to room 504.

"Hang on a sec," I called to Jac.

"Why?" she practically wailed.

My gaze had shifted to the window at the end of the hallway. I began to walk toward it, and I could see that it was closed.

"What are you doing?" Jac called.

I didn't answer her. I reached the window, and tried to open it, but it was locked. I unlatched it, and tried again. The window opened smoothly.

"Kat?"

I ran my hands over the window ledge, then up each side of the window frame.

Just about shoulder height, gouged into the varnish on both sides of the wooden frame, were four scratches. They looked fresh.

Almost as if someone had recently dug their fingers into the window frame.

Chapter 12

After brunch, Jac suggested we take a boat out onto the lake — just the two of us. It was one of those little pedal boats that was shaped like a swan. We pedaled happily in tandem, and the swan obligingly transported us toward the far end of the lake. Halfway there, we both agreed that our legs were getting sore, and we pointed the boat back in the direction of the dock.

It was an incredibly beautiful place. To our left, the massive structure of the Mountain House dwarfed the landscape. To our right, cliffs rose right out of the water, and the towering pine trees on top of them seemed to brush the roof of the world. But the sun that had given me so much comfort when I woke up that morning had disappeared, swallowed up by dark clouds that advanced quickly with the breeze.

"I'm thinking about going to this strings and woodwinds symposium at one o'clock," Jac announced. "But I haven't really decided yet."

I glanced at my watch.

"It's twelve-thirty now," I said. "When exactly are you planning on making this decision?"

Jac's peddling sped up slightly.

"I don't know. Whenever. I guess I'll probably go," she said, staring straight ahead.

I watched her face for a moment, curious.

"Jac," I said, then hesitated to think

about how I should phrase what I wanted to say. "Do you want . . . I mean, if you feel like you . . . uh . . ."

Jac gave me a sharp look.

"What?" she asked. "Spit it out, Voodoo Mama."

"Okay. Here's the thing — you quit the cello big time, during the last convention your mother dragged you to."

"So what are you saying, that I'm not allowed to —," Jac interrupted testily, but I shushed her.

"Let me finish! Okay, so you did that, you took a stand against your mother and that was great. I think you really needed to do that, Jac. Your mom has called the shots about your cello playing all your life, and you had to assert yourself, and you did."

Jac's pedaling slowed slightly. She fiddled with the ring on her left pinky finger.

"Okay, now fast-forward to summer. You went to your mother, and said you might consider coming to this conference, but only if I could come."

Jac nodded.

"And you're spending some time with other young musicians now, kind of getting back into that world a little, and I'm getting the distinct feeling that what all this is about is that you may want to take up the cello again after all."

Jac glared at me.

"So what if I do?" she practically yelled. "Is there some statute of limitations that —"

"Let me *finish*!" I shouted.

Jac looked startled. I didn't shout very often, so I guess she knew I meant business.

"No, there is no statute of limitations on changing your mind about the cello," I said.

"You have every right to make that decision now; in fact, I'm sure it's what everyone was hoping would happen."

"Everyone? You mean you and my mother, who you're suddenly so fond of?" Jac said.

"I mean *everyone*, Jac. Your mom, your teacher Miss Wittencourt, my mom. Me."

Jac twisted the ring on her finger, her brow furrowed.

"This is a good thing, Jac. A fabulous thing. It had to happen this way. You made the break, and now you are coming to realize all by yourself that you *do* want to play the cello.

"I think you finally know what you want, but you feel a little conflicted. You *did* make this huge stand against your mom, and you Quit with a capital Q, and now you've changed your mind. I just think you need to be okay with the fact that you can do something you really want in *spite* of the fact that it pleases your mother."

Jac gave me a funny look.

"Who made you my personal junior psychiatrist?" she asked.

I tried to laugh, even though I knew she meant it as a put-down.

"No one, Maestra. I'm not a junior psychiatrist. I'm your friend. "

Jac pursed her lips.

"So that makes you an expert on what I think," she said. "Because apparently you know what I'm feeling better than I do."

"I'm just giving an opinion. And I'm trying to give you some advice. Forget about your mom, and just go for it. You don't have to pretend not to care about the cello anymore, Jac. It's *your* choice now."

Jac looked at me, scowling.

"Sounds to me more like it's *your* choice this time," Jac stated.

I took a deep breath, trying to control my temper.

"Jac, god. All I'm trying to do is help you. That's all that I want."

Jac started pedaling double-time. The dock was getting closer, but we still had a ways to go.

"See, I'm having trouble believing that," Jac said, between deep breaths. "Because what it's really starting to look like to me is that my mother has won you over to her side. You think I've forgotten how you were hanging out, sipping your designer water and having girl talk yesterday? She's gotten to you somehow, Kat. She's convinced you to be the cello advocate for her. What did she promise you? Invitations to other fancy vacations that your mother could never aff —"

I gasped as Jac cut herself off. It was too late — it had been all too clear where that sentence was going. Jac had never, ever been deliberately cruel to me before, and she'd certainly never brought up the difference in our family's financial situations. Even she looked surprised by what had just come out of her mouth.

"I take that last part back," she said very quietly, hanging her head.

But she was still scowling.

"I don't even know who you are right now," I said, rubbing at my eyes, which had started to fill with tears. "The fact that you could in any seriousness think I'm acting as some kind of secret agent for your mother is beyond insane. Though to tell you the truth, if this is how you act when the subject of your cello comes up, I'm starting to have a little sympathy for her."

"Well you can take her side all that you want!" Jac cried.

"That's just stupid," I retorted.

"Just pedal. I have a symposium to get to, and I don't want to be late."

"And you don't want your hair messed up when Dream Boy and his violin show up."

Jac glared at me.

"I knew it. You're jealous! For once, a beautiful boy is interested in me, and you can't handle it. Did you know that Colin asked me to have a hot chocolate with him after the hike? He *likes* me, Kat, and it's eating you up, because the only person paying any attention to you looks like a caveman and makes fun of mediums."

We had reached the dock. Jac jumped out of the boat first.

I sat with my feet still on the pedals. I was shaking so hard I didn't think I could stand up.

There was a minute when Jac just stood there, when we were kind of looking at each other, though not in the eye. I thought maybe one of us was going to relent. That someone would say something to diffuse the situation, and the fight would be over. But she turned on her heel and headed at top speed for the Mountain House.

I knew that deep down, there was a reason Jac had lashed out at me the way she had, but I didn't care what it was. She had been so unfair, she had been mean, and she had hurt me. Now we were on the outs, and that meant I was on my own. I would have to head inside, and figure out what to do with myself.

Fortunately, I'd packed some very long books.

I walked slowly up the path to the Mountain House. I wanted to give Jac plenty of time to disappear. The last thing I needed was to run into her in the lobby, especially if she was with her music friends. For all I knew, she was trashing me to them this very minute. On second thought, I knew she wouldn't do that. But I still didn't want to see her. I lingered on one of the covered porches, waiting for enough time to pass until I could go inside safely.

I pretended to be engrossed in various announcements that had been posted on the Whispering Pines bulletin board. In the process of trying to look as if I was reading something, the map of the grounds caught my eye.

YOU ARE HERE, proclaimed large letters, with a large red arrow pointing to a spot just outside the Mountain House. I glanced up, half expecting to see the giant red arrow suspended there in midair, pointing helpfully to the porch at my feet.

The map showed the boat launch where Jac and I had gotten the swan boat that had witnessed our argument. It showed the swimming hole, the hiking paths, and the fire tower that I'd visited. The map also showed the other side of the Mountain House grounds, where the gardens were. My eyes were drawn to a marking on the map. LABYRINTH, it said.

I had never been in a real garden labyrinth. I loved the idea of a maze made of plants and hedges. If this labyrinth was on the grand scale of everything else at the Mountain House, it was sure to be spectacular. Maybe Jac and I could —

I stopped the thought. Jac had taken herself out of the picture. Why should I save this experience to share with her?

Taking one final look at the map, I set off on the path that led around the Mountain House so that I could walk the labyrinth alone.

Chapter 13

The labyrinth was beyond the lush gardens of the Mountain House. I was so eager to get there I didn't stop to linger and enjoy the flowers. They would have to wait for another time. I followed the little wooden signs that led to the garden's entrance — a wall of massive hedge with a door-width gap.

When I walked through the entrance, I had the choice of going left or right. I tried left first, walking about fifteen feet until I came to a dead end. I turned around and went in the other direction. From my perspective that way ended in a dead end too — just a wall of green. But when I actually reached the end, I was able to see that the path continued at a right angle.

It was like being in another world. I could see nothing but the deep green of the hedge, and gray sky overhead. I could be anywhere. It could be anytime. There was a strange but not frightening energy in the labyrinth. Maybe it was the energy of plant life, underfoot and all around me. I reached another junction and turned. Dead end. But when I backtracked, I wasn't sure which direction I'd come from.

Just go any old way, I thought. *I'll find something soon.* It was a public labyrinth after all, for the guests. It couldn't be that hard. The Mountain House didn't want to lose paying guests in a hedgy maze. That would be bad for business.

I was starting to feel a little uncomfortable, though. Seriously, which direction had I come from? Maybe I really could get lost in this thing. How long before anyone would even know I was missing? And would anyone think to come here?

I heard a giggle, and I whirled around.

There was a little girl standing about ten feet away from me. She had on a neat white dress with petticoats, and looked unusually clear with an electric air about her. She held an orange kitten in her arms.

A ghost.

She giggled again, and dashed off to her left, disappearing into what looked like solid green. After a moment, I went to the place she'd been standing. It was not a solid wall of green after all — there was a low doorway cut in the hedge. I went through, and saw the girl again. She was walking away from me, but she paused and looked over her shoulder. She had the brightest red hair I'd ever seen, and wide laughing blue eyes. She made a turn, and I quickly followed her.

Another low doorway.

I hope this isn't one of those prankster ghosts, I thought, ducking through the gap where she had gone. *She might be trying to show me the way, but she might just as well be trying to get me more lost.* For all I knew the girl had died in the labyrinth, and was looking for some eternal company.

Now she was at the far end of the leafy corridor. She squealed as she caught sight of me, as if thrilled to have gotten me in the game. When she moved off, I tailed her again. This time there was no low doorway, but an optical illusion of flat hedge that on closer examination was one wall just in front of another one. You would really have to know it was there to push between the two walls, but once there it was obvious there was a small path.

I could no longer see the girl but could still hear her laughing. There was only one way to go now, doubling back down another short path. When I reached the end, I came out into an open, circular space. At its center was a stone bench, and someone was sitting on it.

But it wasn't the redheaded girl.

"Oh! How did you get in here?"

It was a woman about my mother's age, with brown hair in a "sensible" short cut. She was holding a book, and wearing faded jeans and a denim shirt with a Whispering Pines employee badge. Definitely alive and breathing.

"I don't really know," I said. "I got turned around. I'm sorry — am I not supposed to be here?"

The woman closed her book and stood up.

"No, it's fine, really," she said. "It's just that I've never had a guest find their way here before. This is an annex of the main labyrinth — sort of a Mountain House secret. There's a hidden entrance off one of the main passages that leads away from the regular path. I come here to read sometimes."

"I'll go back," I said, though I had significant doubts I could do so without the little girl's help.

"No, come take a load off," the woman said, patting the stone bench next to her. "I've read this book before, anyway. Besides, you might not find your way out. The main labyrinth is pretty idiotproof, but you can really get lost in the annex."

Relieved, I sat down next to her. Something about her reminded me of my mother, with the exception of the "mom" haircut.

"I'm Kat," I said. "Room 505."

"Alex," she said. "Accounting and Reservations."

We grinned at each other, and my feeling of liking her was reinforced. Though I'm the most sensitive to dead people, sometimes I get feelings about living people, too. My gut was telling me that Alex was good people.

"I'm actually relieved to see you," Alex said. "I was sitting here reading, and I thought I heard a laugh from just on the other side of the hedge there. Started wondering if I was hearing things, or I'd read one too many of my Spiritualist books."

Interesting, I thought. Alex must be somewhat sensitive, spirit-wise, to have heard that laugh. Because it hadn't come from me.

"Spiritualist books?" I asked.

She showed me the cover of the book in her hands. The title was *The Spiritualists in America*.

"I've always been fascinated with this period in history," Alex said. "Especially the Spiritualists. Plus there's a link to the Mountain House, so it's doubly cool. That's actually how I got interested in the Spiritualists, because of this place. Do you know about them?"

I didn't respond, but kept an open, curious expression on my face so that she'd keep talking.

"Probably not — I guess it's a pretty obscure topic these days. They were sort of the first mediums in this country. One of them lived at the Mountain House for a time."

I loved that Alex was giving no disclaimers. I also loved that the red-haired girl had led me directly to someone else that might know something about Madame Serena.

"I know a little bit about them," I said. "There was this guy who worked here, actually one of *the* Mountain House family, la-dee-dah and all that, who started telling me about the Spiritualists. But he was really condescending about it, you know, all 'how stupid is this' and everything. I wanted to throttle him. So, I never really got the story. Something about the Foxes?"

Alex had been giving me a lopsided smile while I talked, but now she broke into a full grin.

"The Fox sisters. I think I've read everything ever written about them. Maggie and Katy started contacting spirits in the 1840s when they were barely into their teens. At first, only their family knew about it, but word spread, and friends and neighbors starting dropping by. They would ask questions, and these loud knocking and rapping sounds would answer them, always using the two girls as conduits. Maggie figured out a way to ask the spirits yes and no questions and translate the responses. Nobody could find any explanation for how this was happening. People came up with all kinds of tests, making the girls stand on boxes or holding their hands during the raps. No one could even produce a theory as to how a teenage girl could create a sound like that on demand. Everybody agreed the sisters were the real deal. They were contacting spirits.

"Word spread like wildfire. Thousands of people witnessed Maggie and Katy's spirit communications. Before long they were celebrities, not just in America but in Europe, too. A huge community followed them, and other mediums stepped forward. And that's how the Spiritualist movement was born, and Maggie Fox was its leader. Until one day, in 1888 — that's after forty years of working as a world-renowned medium, mind you — Maggie suddenly went public and claimed her entire career had been an elaborate hoax."

"What?" I cried.

Alex nodded.

"I know, right? Well, Maggie claimed it had all started as a prank, after she and Katy found that they could crack the bones in their feet to make loud popping sounds. She said they invented a story about a murdered peddler in their house, then told their parents as a joke, and 'contacted' the peddler to make it scary. When their friends and neighbors started filing in to witness what was going on, their older sister Leah encouraged them to keep doing it. I'm guessing she smelled money.

"Anyway, practically before they knew it half the country had heard of the Fox sisters and the famous 'spook house' where they lived. Maggie and Katy started holding public séances and charging for them. The money poured in, and soon they were supporting the entire family. Maggie kept on doing so for forty years. Until all at once she apparently felt compelled to come forward and tell the world it had all been an act — a lie."

I shook my head.

"But why would she do that? You said people tried to prove she was faking, and no one could," I said.

Alex nodded.

"To this day I guess no one really knows

for certain why she did it. The whole Spiritualist community was just devastated by her announcement. It made front-page headlines all over the country, and everyone took Maggie's statement to mean that all of Spiritualism was a lie — that all the people earning livings as mediums were basically criminals. It created this massive shockwave throughout the country.

"The thing is, there were some mediums who actually were fakers. There was a very famous one named Madame Diss De Barr, who rigged up these elaborate mechanisms to simulate spirits, and she got caught doing it. I think that was right around the time of Maggie's announcement. And the crazy thing is, Maggie didn't stop there. A year later just as the storm was dying down, she was in the headlines again. This time she claimed she'd been the real thing all along, and her claim of it all being a hoax was a lie. But . . . there's so much more about her that plays into it. If you're interested in her, I have a little biography of her I could lend you."

I nodded.

"But what do you think? Which was the truth? I mean, you've read so much about them and everything. Do you think Maggie was faking . . . or . . ."

Alex gave me another crooked grin.

"Or was she faking that she was faking?" she finished my question for me.

I nodded again.

"I can't deny I have a theory about that," Alex said. "But you should decide for yourself. If you're interested."

"Oh, I am!" I said quickly. "I mean, you've piqued my curiosity."

"Tell you what," Alex said. "I'll leave the book in an envelope at the front desk with

your room number on it. It's really short —
not even a hundred pages. And there are bits
about other mediums you can skip if you
want. Just skim through it, and see what you
think."

"I will," I said eagerly. I almost asked her
if we could go and get the book right away. I
had time to kill, now that Jac and I were fighting. Plus the clouds had gotten much darker.
A raindrop landed on the stone bench between us.

"Here it comes," Alex said. "We'd better
go before the skies open. Up here on the
mountain, the weather can go from zero to
eighty in three seconds flat."

She got up and headed for a spot in the
hedge. Even now, I couldn't tell where the
gap was where I'd entered the circle. But
Alex knew, and she was moving fast, and I
made sure to keep up.

She trotted at a brisk pace, making sudden turns, ducking under the low doorways that didn't seem to be there until she disappeared through them. I looked over my shoulder a few times, and once I thought I caught a glimpse of a white skirt. I sent a silent "Thank you" in the direction of the little girl. She was clearly happiest staying right where she was, in the heart of the garden maze.

In about half the time it took me to get in, we were standing outside the labyrinth. Fat raindrops had started falling.

"You better sprint for it," Alex said. "I've got to run to the parking lot and close the windows in my car. I'll leave the book for you. Remember to look for it."

"I will, definitely!" I said. "Thanks, Alex."

She smiled and nodded, and just before I

turned to bolt for the Mountain House my eye dropped to her name tag.

It read Alex Kenyon. Of the Whispering Pines Kenyons, I presumed. I winced with embarrassment as I turned, remembering what I'd said about Ted.

Lah-dee-DUH.

Chapter 14

I tried to put my embarrassing statements out of my mind as I dashed into the hotel, but I couldn't help dwelling on it. Alex probably thought I was making fun of the whole Kenyon family, when I was really just making fun of Ted. Although I didn't know which was worse. What an idiot I was.

Earlier in the day I'd glimpsed a big reading room on the main floor, with armchairs and a fireplace. I could think of worse things to do than curl up with a good book near a roaring fire on a rainy afternoon, and it might take my mind off my faux pas with Alex. I decided to go up to my room and get one of the novels I'd packed.

When I got to the fifth-floor hallway, I could see that there was something leaning up against my door. It was a large black book with an envelope taped to the front. I picked it up, unlocked my door, and went inside. I sat on my bed, pulled the envelope off the book, and took out the card inside.

Dear Kat,

I looked your name up in the register to find your room number. I hope that's okay. I wanted to apologize for my rudeness last night. You were absolutely right to be angry with me. What I said was thoughtless and patronizing, and truth be told it was not even representative of my real beliefs on the subject. I hope that you'll accept my apology.

I took the liberty of pulling the scrapbook I mentioned to you, the volume that contains information on Madame Serena. Our hotel scrapbooks have been organized by year, and in this volume you'll find all of what has been preserved in connection with Madame Serena. I hope it is helpful to you.

Yours sincerely,
Ted Kenyon

I read the note through a second time. I was surprised by it, because after last night I was sure I'd seen the last of Ted Kenyon. However obnoxious he'd been, it said something about him that he'd taken the trouble to find my room and write a note of apology. And more, that he'd gotten the scrapbook for me. Impressive.

I put the note aside, stretched out on my bed, and opened the scrapbook. It was chock-full of newspaper clippings and photographs from the year 1888.

The Mountain House had added a wing and built the labyrinth in 1888, and many of the first newspaper articles and photographs documented that. There were faded, handwritten letters in elegant writing from guests, thanking the Mountain House for their wonderful stays. There was a dinner menu, which revealed that every night when they dined, men were expected to wear black tie and women evening dress.

I almost forgot about Madame Serena as I pored over the old photographs. Though more additions had been built onto the hotel since then, much of what was pictured looked very similar to the way it was now. I squinted at a photograph of an elegant family posing at the very boat dock where Jac and I had just parted. Except for the formal

Victorian clothing, the picture could have been taken yesterday.

I turned the page and took a quick breath in as a very familiar face appeared. There was Madame Serena, turban and all. It was a newspaper clipping from May of 1888. The headline read *Spiritualist Movement Reaches Whispering Pines with the Arrival of Medium Madame Serena.* There was a short article stating that Madame Serena would be coming to take up residence at the Mountain House for an indefinite period of time, during which she would make her abilities available to the general public for a modest fee.

On the next page there was a small ad featuring Madame Serena looking mystical and ethereal in her turban. If this was all Ted had to go on when it came to judging mediums, maybe it wasn't so surprising he thought mocking them was the safest bet.

Madame Serena, from my twenty-first-century perspective, did look a bit silly. I smiled at her picture, though. For all her theatrical ways and her deaf insistence on calling me Simple Cat, I kind of liked her.

The next thing I came across was a number of newspaper clippings from September 1888. A large headline declared *Shocked Spiritualists Stunned by Maggie Fox's Exposé.* Another screamed *Renowned Medium Confesses Hoax — Famous Fox Sister States Spiritualism a Fraud!*

This was exactly what Alex had been talking about. It couldn't be a coincidence she had known so much about it. Maybe it was the contents of this very album that had gotten her so interested in the Spiritualists. Losing all track of time, I absorbed myself in reading every word of the articles.

The local newspapers reported that Maggie Fox's revelation had stunned and angered the country, and devastated the Spiritualist community. Both of the articles mentioned that the owners of the Whispering Pines Mountain House were concerned by the news, since a Spiritualist medium was residing and doing business there. I guess that's why they were included in the scrapbook. Someone named Agatha Kenyon was quoted as saying that she would be recommending to the Kenyon men that all Spiritualists, including Madame Serena, be henceforth banned from the Mountain House.

There was one other article that caught my eye, a short one. The headline read *Skepticism Greets Madame Serena in the Wake of the Fox Scandal.* The article recapped Maggie Fox's confession, and related that as the country began to reject the Spiritualists, the local community had turned against Madame Serena, calling her a fraud and a criminal. It mentioned Agatha Kenyon's threat to ban all Spiritualists from the Mountain House, and said that all of Madame Serena's clients had abandoned her save for one.

I sat up and read the article through again. It was dated December 14th, 1888. There were no other articles in the scrapbook about Madame Serena or the Spiritualists. Based on all that I'd read, and based on what Madame Serena herself had told me, I had a more complete idea of why she was stuck here, and the climate surrounding her final days.

Pleased with myself, I leafed through the last few pages of the scrapbook again, and this time I saw something I hadn't noticed before. It looked as if the article had been ripped out of the scrapbook, then taped back in, then partially ripped out a second time. I could make out the headline.

Murder at Whispering Pines — a Diabolical Act on the Famous Resort's Fifth Floor.

The article had been torn out several lines below the heading. I was only able to make out that a female guest of the hotel had been murdered. It didn't give the woman's name, or the number of the room in which she'd been killed, or any other details. Whatever else the newspaper had to report had been long since torn away.

But I knew perfectly well which room it was.

Chapter 15

The weather went from bad to worse — the sky was an ominous gray-green, and the rain had turned into a heavy downpour.

I grabbed one of my books and went in search of the reading room and its fireplace. Every time I explored the main floor, another room or corridor seemed to pop up that I'd never seen before. The floor plan resembled a well-played Scrabble game, with stuff tacked on in any direction it could be squashed in.

I was enjoying exploring, and deliberately chose not to ask an employee how to get to the reading room. It was more fun blundering around on my own. It made me think of Lucy and her siblings exploring the big country house in *The Lion, the Witch, and the Wardrobe.*

During my search, I passed a set of glass double doors with curtains. I could tell from the strains of music coming from inside that it was the location of Jac's symposium. I quickly banished thoughts of my best friend from my mind.

I found the reading room at the very end of the hall. It was exactly as I'd pictured it — a kind of plush, Victorian library with lots of massive armchairs and couches and a really good fire going in the hearth. I could see there was a good seat very close to the fire, and I happily made my way over to it. When

I was almost there, I glanced in the direction of a sound, and saw two people sitting snugly on a love seat by the window.

The girl was blond and smiley and wore a pink sweater set. A living Barbie doll.

The boy was Colin.

I immediately looked away. I didn't want them to think I'd seen them. But if I turned around now and walked back past them to leave the room, I would call attention to myself. Instead, I claimed the comfy seat near the fire, and curled myself in it so that I was facing in the other direction.

Colin and definitely-not-Jac. Cleo the clarinet player perhaps?

Jac was going to be devastated.

Jac had seemed so sure that the two of them were becoming an item. Was I supposed to tell her about this? It would be useless at this point — Jac would probably assume I'd made the whole thing up to get back at her.

Don't think about it right now, I told myself. *You can't change it, and you can't make it better for Jac. It is what it is. Put it out of your mind, and read.*

Obedient to the voice in my head, I opened my book and read the first sentence four or five times, without really absorbing it. I was giving it a sixth try when I sensed someone was approaching me. This was insane. Would Dream Boy actually come over with his Barbie, knowing I was Jac's friend?

"Hey. Sorry to interrupt. Say the word and I'm gone."

I looked up to see Ted standing over me, looking sheepish and appearing especially Cro-Magnonish in the firelight.

"Oh," I exclaimed. "I mean, no. Sorry. I thought you were someone else."

Ted looked anxious.

"So I should go then. That's cool, Kat. I understand, seriously."

"That's not what I meant," I said, more quickly than I intended to. "I mean, it's fine, Ted. You don't have to go."

He looked hugely relieved. There was a little footstool next to the fireplace, and he pulled it over and sat down next to me.

"Did you get the book I left you?"

"Yeah, I did. That was really nice of you — you didn't have to do that. But it was really interesting."

"Did you see the stuff about Madame Serena?" he asked.

"Uh-huh."

Ted paused, looking uncomfortable.

"Like I said in the note," he began, then his voice faltered.

"Ted, it's fine."

"What I really wanted was to apologize to you in person," Ted said.

His look was so earnest I couldn't help smiling.

"I think you just did," I said.

"I'm not like that," he said. "I mean, what I said about mediums. I was just blabbering. I was trying to be . . . convivial."

"Convivial?" I asked.

"It's something they teach us here — when we work the Mountain House, we're not just learning the ropes of running the business, we're supposed to be learning people skills."

Ah. Ted might want to consider taking some extra classes.

"We're supposed to get along with everybody. And sometimes that means hiding who we are to be more of a generic Joe Blow who agrees with everything you say kind of a guy. And for some reason I thought the generic Joe Blow response to the Spiritualists was to laugh at them. I just assumed. It was obviously the worst thing to do. And ironically, that's totally not how I was raised."

"It's okay," I said. "I have . . . my family is . . . oh, it's complicated. I just have reason to know that people involved with paranormal stuff, whoever they are — researchers or mediums or healers or whatever — that they are way more regular than you think. They're not Madame Serena. They're people."

"Of course," Ted said quickly.

"Anyway . . . ," my voice trailed off. It was the preferred Brooklyn Bigelow method of indicating a subject change. I hated to give credit to Brooklyn for anything, but it worked like a charm.

"There are other scrapbooks, and plenty of papers and photos, if you're interested," Ted said. "My mother wrote her doctoral thesis on the Spiritualists — so we have a lot of books about them."

"What do you know about Maggie Fox?" I asked.

"Oh, gosh. Margaret Fox. My mom would —"

Ted was interrupted by a huge clap of thunder outside. The lights flickered, then went out.

"Oh no," he said, getting to his feet. "We've lost power. Our generator is being repaired — the timing couldn't be worse. I'm sorry, Kat, but they're going to need extra hands at the front desk. This could be a massive headache. The guests will be freaking out. I mean . . . some of the guests. Not you, obviously."

I smiled.

"Go. Good luck," I said.

"I'll find you later," he called, then sprinted for the door.

"You don't have to," I wanted to call after him. Though in truth the Cro-Magnon Boy was starting to grow on me a little.

I heard a giggle. I discreetly peered over my shoulder. The Barbie had responded to the loss of power by snuggling up to Colin in mock terror. How ridiculous. It was the middle of the day, after all. It wasn't like the Mountain House had been plunged into darkness.

I decided to bail on the reading room. I couldn't concentrate with the lovebirds cuddling in the corner, and witnessing it made me feel disloyal to Jac. And something had occurred to me. A power outage is an excellent time to have a séance.

All of the electronic stuff we use has the effect of messing up the electric field, making it harder for spirit activity to come through to our physical plane. That's why séances are usually held in the dark and at night, when many electronics are switched off. This might be the perfect time to communicate with Madame Serena, and help her out of her time loop.

I arrived at my room slightly breathless, since the lack of power meant I had to walk up five flights of stairs. I unlocked my door, went in, and sat on the bed. I opened my mind to the sounds and sensations of being in the room, focusing on the rain, the thunder, and the smell of the storm until I was completely in the moment.

It's hard to describe exactly what I do mentally and energetically when I'm trying to communicate with a spirit. Usually, the spirits just come to me, and I react to them. But sometimes I need to reach a spirit that isn't currently manifesting. I kind of imagine myself as a satellite dish, and I broadcast a call to the person I'm trying to reach. I transmit the signal in every direction. And I wait.

This time, it didn't take long. Madame Serena blinked into reality right next to me, as smoothly as if she'd just beamed down from the Starship *Enterprise*.

She didn't seem to notice I was there, probably because she was too intent on "raising" me herself, her eyes closed and her lips moving in a silent chant.

"Hi," I said.

She didn't hear me.

"I'm here," I said, a little louder.

Her eyes opened, and her hand flew to her chest.

"Simple Cat!"

Ah. Whatever.

"Hello," I said. "I'm glad you're here, Madame Serena."

She bowed her head.

"I am honored, Simple Cat. Thank you for coming. The Colonel's wife isn't here yet, but I'm sure she will be along shortly. How gratifying it will be to tell her you have come to our circle. She has been so patient in waiting to see Loretta — she had never accused me, like the others, never . . ."

"Madame Serena, I need you to listen to me," I said.

She looked at me, wide-eyed, like I was about to levitate.

"You have been here before," I said.

"This is my room," Madame Serena replied. "Of course I've been here before, Simple Cat."

"In this moment. Don't you realize it? You have been in this moment many times before."

She looked perplexed.

"Madame Serena, I'm not a spirit," I explained carefully.

"But you are here, in my circle," Madame Serena exclaimed. "I summoned you! You are the Guardian of the Sacred Portal of Transmigration. You are a spirit."

"I'm not," I said. "But the thing of it is, one of us is."

Madame Serena said nothing, just stared at me, her hands shaking slightly.

"Let me explain a little," I said.

I was really stalling for time. This was the first time I had to look a spirit in the eyes and tell it like it was. I couldn't just blurt out "You're dead."

"Madame Serena, your . . . essence is . . .

no longer fully focused in physical reality," I said.

She stared.

"You have departed," I offered.

She stared.

"You've passed on," I whispered.

"Simple Cat, you speak cryptically, and I cannot take your meaning," Madame Serena stated.

"You're dead," I said, louder than I meant to. I guess being blunt was the way to go after all.

Madame Serena drew slightly away from me.

"Simple Cat?"

I couldn't read her expression.

"I'm a medium," I told her. "Like you . . . were. And the year is . . . well, it's not even the 1900s any more. Quite a bit of time has passed. You appeared to me outside the

Mountain House, then again here in this room. No one else can see you. Not even the bellboy. But I can. You're stuck in a moment in time, Madame Serena. But I can help you to move on to the other side."

"I'm dead?" Madame Serena asked, incredulously.

My eyes filled with tears. This was horrible! I hated it! What kind of a thing was this to have to do to somebody — tell them they'd kicked off?

"You are," I said very gently. "You're dead, Madame Serena."

She took a long, deep breath, clasping her hands together. I braced myself. If the furniture was going to fly, it would be now.

"But that's . . . *wonderful!*" Madame Serena cried.

"I . . . it is?"

"I have longed for ages to see the Summerland," Madame Serena said, pressing the back of one hand to her forehead. "Everyone in this life that I have loved has preceded me there. I have no one left in this world. The Colonel's wife is the only one who cares for me at all. I have no one else — not a soul. Perhaps that is why I have tried for so many years to lift the veil to the spirit world. "

Her eyes clouded slightly.

"But ... surely this isn't ... I'm not in the Summerland, am I?"

I shook my head.

"You haven't crossed over, Madame Serena. Something is connecting you to the Mountain House. And I think I may know what it is."

Madame Serena looked at me eagerly.

"Oh speak to me, Simple Cat," she said.

I grinned.

"You came to the Mountain House and

lived in this room," I said. "You had been holding séances here for months when Maggie Fox made her public confession that all of Spiritualism was a fraud."

Her face darkened.

"Dreadful day," she said. "Loathsome woman. How could she have done it?"

"I don't know," I said. "But not too long afterwards, people stopped coming to see you. They didn't believe anymore."

"They called me a hoax monger and a deceiver," Madame Serena said, her voice wavering. "You see all, Simple Cat, so I know that you see the truth about me. During all my séances at the Mountain House, I have never successfully made full contact with the spirit world. But I never pretended to — I never lied! Never rigged tricks like that dreadful Madame Diss De Barr and her loathsome deceptions. I only persevered because I came so close — because I truly believed that I could contact the spirit world, under the right conditions."

"I know you aren't a liar," I told Madame Serena. And I was secretly relieved to learn that she wasn't a fraud. I had grown to like Madame Serena very much.

"In the end, only the Colonel's wife stood by me," Madame Serena said forlornly. "Poor creature — losing Loretta almost destroyed her. She needed me. And I would not have led her on, Simple Cat, but that we came so close so many times to succeeding. The door would begin to open — I would sense that Loretta was approaching. But always, Simple Cat, always something happened that caused Loretta to flee."

"What would happen?" I asked.

An expression of fear crossed Madame Serena's face. She leaned closer to me. I could feel the energy coming off her — like a field of static electricity that made my hair stand on end.

"I hardly know how to tell you," she whispered. "But it always came the same way. I would begin to sense Loretta, then the darkness would roll in, like a storm cloud. Like a thunderhead."

A black cloud.

"Could you see this thing?" I asked her.

Madame Serena nodded.

"Somewhat," she said. "It was as if an area of darkness was moving through the room. It had a powerful sense of evil about it, Simple Cat. So much so that each time I felt compelled to cut off contact and end the séance immediately."

Just hearing Madame Serena describe the thing gave me the chills. I recalled all too vividly the sensation of being pushed roughly toward the window. My heart began to race, and my palms grew cold and damp.

I realized all at once that it was no mere memory causing the shivers running up my spine. It knew, somehow. It had heard.

The black cloud was coming.

The black cloud was here.

"Away!" I heard Madame Serena shout. "Simple Cat, protect yourself! Close the portal!"

"I don't know anything about a portal — I didn't do anything!" I cried.

Everything seemed to happen in a blur. Something was coming into focus by the foot of the bed, an inky entity that buzzed like a swarm of flies and seemed to suck the light and the life right out of the room. And just as it had happened in the hall last night — during what I now realized was not a dream — I became paralyzed.

I couldn't move a muscle. I understood perfectly well that I was in terrible danger, that when Madame Serena told me to protect myself she meant it quite literally. But I couldn't move a muscle. There wasn't a thing I could do to help myself.

Then Madame Serena was moving past me — I had no idea a woman of that age and size could move so fast even in spirit form — and she seemed to be throwing herself between me and the black cloud.

Though it was shapeless and eyeless, it had intelligence, and it had understanding. Right now, on the bed where I was sitting frozen like an icicle, the thing could see me. And it didn't like me.

It didn't like me at all.

Chapter 16

When Madame Serena put herself between me and the thing, the spell of paralysis was broken. Somehow I got myself out of the room and into the hallway. My mind was reeling. So much was happening at once.

Madame Serena had seen the black cloud.

The black cloud had seen me.

Madame Serena had provided the power to help me break free.

I ran down the hallway, down five flights

of stairs, and through the lobby, never stopping to catch my breath. I didn't so much as slow down until I came to a door leading to one of the many small covered porches on the first floor.

Somehow being outdoors, even if I was only ten feet from the door, made me feel safer. I sat down heavily in a chair, gasping for breath. Thought after thought raced through my brain.

I had to keep calm and figure out what was happening. I couldn't deal with the situation or protect myself until I understood it better. After I caught my breath, and my heart rate slowed, I tried to go over the puzzle pieces in my mind, and to fit them together one by one.

The black cloud could attack living people. No, not all living people. Living people who could see it or sense it. Somehow, the black cloud must operate on sensitive humans like water did in a tiny chink in a dam. A little would get in, then a little more, until the way in was blasted wide open. That was it.

Madame Serena had lived in room 505.

A woman had been murdered in room 504.

Think, I told myself.

I was a medium. Madame Serena was one, too. She believed she had failed as a medium, but in reality I knew that wasn't true. She had seen the black cloud. It had somehow interfered with her attempts to contact Loretta. So, Madame Serena was the real deal after all.

She'll be so happy when I tell her, I thought.

So the three of us — me, Madame Serena, and the murdered woman in room 504 — had a common link. I knew what I had in common with Madame Serena: we were both sensitive to the spirit world. How did that relate to the woman in room 504? The black cloud couldn't kill a person.

Could it?

I couldn't think this out, and I didn't have enough experience to get any further. I needed help.

I pulled out my cell phone. I only had one bar of reception. And only two bars of battery power. Hopefully that was enough. I dialed my home number.

No answer. My mom wasn't home, or she was in a session. And she didn't have a cell phone.

But I needed help *now*. I'd gotten away from the black cloud twice. Who knew if I'd be so lucky the next time it came for me? And I couldn't stay outside all day.

I pulled up the contacts list on my phone

menu, and found Orin's number. I selected it and hit send, taking a deep breath and hoping this wouldn't be too weird for him.

Orin was an old friend of my mom's who'd recently come back into her life. He was a healer and really smart about supernatural stuff. He was also pretty cute.

Orin had been really helpful to me when I'd started suffering spirit-induced panic attacks in the spring. Since I'd come into my spirit sight, I'd attracted quite a following of ghosts who wanted my attention. When I realized I had a virtual village of spooks surrounding me at all times, I freaked out. But Orin had been able to teach me how to create a private space of energy around me that they couldn't penetrate.

Maybe he'd have some insight into the black cloud.

"Hello?"

"I'm really sorry to bother you," I said, without identifying myself.

"Kat?" Orin asked.

"I can call back later if you're busy."

"I'm not busy. Is everything okay? Are you still with Jac? Did something happen?"

It was kind of nice that he sounded so concerned. I found it a little comforting. Especially given the fact that Jac and I had a huge fight, and were probably not speaking to each other.

"I'm still at the Mountain House, yeah. I just — I need some advice, Orin, and I can't get hold of my mom."

"What's up?" he asked.

I told him, as concisely as I could, about the black cloud. When I finished, there was a long silence on the phone.

"Orin?" I asked. "Are you still there?"

"I'm here, Kat," he said. "I'm just processing what you've told me. I think you need to be very, very careful."

That much I had already worked out, thank you.

"What do you think it is?" I asked.

"I'm guessing, because I haven't seen it. But there are other types of entities than ghosts, Kat. Things that have never been human. Some of them are light beings that have a relationship with humans in order to help them. Some people call them angels, or guides."

"Right," I said.

"But some of them are dark. They look for vulnerable people, or people who give them some kind of opening, so they can get in."

"Get in and do what?" I asked.

"Leech on to an individual. Steal energy. Maybe even take over the person, turn them to their purposes."

"Orin, what are you saying? What is this thing?"

"I think based on what you've told me, it could be some kind of negative entity."

"Like a demon?" I asked, my voice shaking.

"That's just a word, Kat," Orin said. "Not everyone would call it that. I don't even know if I believe in demons. This is a negative entity of some kind. It's not your friend. It's not something that has ever been human. An entity like this can go after a person in two ways. If the person is weak for some reason, the entity could gradually take control of a portion of their personality. It could encourage that person to behave violently. Everyone has free will, mind you. But if the entity could find someone weak — someone who didn't need too much of a push to become a violent person — it would try to take advantage of that person. Take control."

"You mean possession, don't you," I said, the very word sending a chill up my spine. "You're talking about an entity that can posses a person."

"Possibly. There's no black or white, here, Kat. A person couldn't just be taken over completely against his or her will. The violent impulses have to be there already. But in a subtle way, yes. I'm guessing this is the kind of entity that could have a powerfully persuasive force on a vulnerable human being."

"So the woman in the room wasn't murdered by the black cloud."

"Not directly, no. She was probably with someone else. Someone who was already unstable, and the entity knew it and brought it under its control. Urged it to harm her. That would be one way for it to feed."

I swallowed. "What would the other way for the entity to feed be?"

"The other way would be through someone who is psychically open to the spirit world," Orin said very quietly.

"A medium," I said. "Me."

"There was a pretty famous case once . . . this reminds me of it. An entity based in the top floor of a house in Connecticut. These things don't seem to travel — they're specific to a certain location, and they have to take what comes. And they tend to stay exactly where their last host left them. An entity could wait for centuries for a vulnerable human to cross its path."

"But in a hotel . . ."

"A much bigger selection, yes," Orin said. "This thing in the Connecticut house, it had been thought by some to be responsible for the previous owner's madness. The man had always been unpleasant, but one night he went over the edge. The next owner of the house, a lady who turned out to be very slightly sensitive psychically — just felt there was something wrong with the bedroom. She felt sick when she was there — she got headaches and felt on edge."

Like Jac's mom, I thought. Which meant she was slightly psychic too. And she didn't even know it.

"So she called in a medium — I know the guy, actually. He could sense the entity, and the thing knew it. It went straight at him in a full-out attack. Because he had opened himself to receive spirit energy, the thing was able to jump right into him. Tried to get him to throw himself down a staircase."

I had a chilling memory of the black

cloud pushing me toward the window. I told Orin about it.

"So did that really happen to me, or did I dream it?" I asked.

"Both, I think," Orin said. "You were already in tune with the thing, and sensing it in your sleep. Human spirits can leave their bodies during sleep — it's very natural — most of us do it all the time and never know it. You would have been incredibly vulnerable to it, Kat, if you were in that state, out of your body on the astral plane, and it came at you."

"But it didn't get me. I used the energy blocks you taught me, and somehow I got away," I said, my voice wavering.

I wanted Orin to tell me that I was safe now. That I had proved my power — that I wasn't in danger.

"Kat, this thing has seen you, and come at you. It's got you in its sights now. Because of your psychic abilities, you're directly vulnerable to it, and I'm not certain you have the full power to protect yourself every time it attacks. I'm not sure any living person does. And I do believe it will be back."

"What about someone who *isn't* living?" I asked.

"What do you mean?" he asked.

I told him about Madame Serena.

"She threw herself at it and suddenly I could move again," I told him. "That's how I got away the second time."

"Interesting," Orin said. "Here's the thing. An entity like this feeds by manipulating a living human — through their body. Madame Serena is no longer living. So she can sense the thing and fight it, and it isn't as good fighting her off, because she doesn't have a physical form to manipulate."

"So she can protect me."

"She did once. Who can say if she can do it again? It sounds like it comes after you, not her. What if she isn't around the next time? Kat, I'm very concerned. I think we have to get ahold of your mother. I don't want you to take this on alone."

"No offense, Orin, but I don't think I have much of a choice. I'm here, and so is the black cloud. And like you said, it has me in its sights now. What if Madame Serena and I work together? Is there a way to get rid of an entity like this?"

Orin sighed.

"It's possible. But I don't want you to go looking for this thing."

"Better me looking for it, than it looking for me. Just tell me what to do," I said. "If it came back. You said it was possible to get rid of something like this. How?"

"I can only tell you what worked for my friend in Connecticut," Orin said anxiously. "Your mother is the expert. I'm just guessing the entity in that hotel functions the same way as the one in the Connecticut house. I can only go from that."

"It's going to have to be good enough," I said. "Please, Orin. Just tell me what you know."

"Well, the key is light, Kat," he said. "Light in every form is this thing's enemy. When you read about the forces of dark and light, whether it's in a cultural myth or in *Star Wars*, the metaphor is quite literal. Light energy is the energy of love, of goodness, and of beneficence. Dark energy is the energy of hatred and destruction.

"A person, no matter how weak, could protect themselves from being entered physically with a simple prayer or call to whatever power they believe in, if only they knew to do it. But it's coming at you psychically, and that's much harder to block. You need to hit it with every form of light you can — call on all the Beings of Light that the Universe can put at your disposal, then bombard it with light energy, which you'll have to visualize. Think of a star going super nova. And throw love at it. Every caring, compassionate emotion you can muster.

"It feeds on fear. No matter how scared you feel, replace it with the image of something or someone that inspires pure love in you. And not to be obvious, but keep every light in your room switched on."

Now that was a problem at the moment. But there was no point in mentioning it — it would only make Orin more anxious.

"Okay," I said. "And how will I know? If I've gotten rid of it, I mean?"

"I don't know," Orin said, sighing. "I can only guess that you *will* know. But Kat . . ."

"And if I don't get rid of it, it will still be there, right, Orin? The next time someone checks into that room, or even visits some-one in that room, it will be there. Trying to get into them."

"I . . . yes. It might."

"Jac's mom is staying in that room, Orin. And she already sensed something. She gets headaches, and she's not herself."

"Kat, listen to me. I'm going to drive over to your house to find your mom. I want you to talk to her directly."

"I'm all for it," I said. "I just need to make sure I can handle myself now. In case."

"Be careful," Orin said.

"I will. I promise."

"You better," he said. "Be well, Kat. Stay in the light."

I said good-bye and hung up.

Orin had done as much to prepare me as possible. Now I was on my own.

I felt sick to my stomach.

I was also terrified to the bone.

Chapter 17

I went back inside, uncertain what to do next. I wasn't too keen on going back upstairs after what had just happened. The best thing to do seemed to be to wait until my mother called me. I checked my phone, and groaned in dismay.

The low battery light was flashing. I probably had less than an hour left on it if I didn't make any calls.

I decided to switch the phone off. If an emergency came up, I could try to make another call. If I left it on waiting for my mom, it might run out of juice before she had a chance to reach me. And I couldn't recharge it until the electricity came back on.

I was back in the same situation as after lunch. It was raining, I had nothing to do, and Jac was in cello-land. I also realized that I'd left my book somewhere — probably in my comfy seat in the reading room. I decided to go and get it and then look for a Barbie and Colin–free zone to read until Jac's symposium got out.

The book was exactly where I thought I'd left it, and the lovebirds were nowhere to be seen. I was heading through the main lobby when I saw Jac's mom at the front desk.

"Tylenol is fine," she was saying, taking a little packet from the woman behind the lobby desk.

"Mrs. Gray," I said, walking toward her.

She turned to face me. She had dark circles under her eyes. Her face was blank for a moment, like she didn't know me. I found it very unnerving.

"Jac's at the strings and woodwind symposium," I told her. I felt it was the one sentence in the universe that might cause her to smile. But she just stared at me, like she thought I'd been a dream and now here I was in real life.

She fingered the Tylenol packet in her hand.

"So you still have a headache?" I asked.

"Obviously," she barked, then pressed her hand to her forehead. "I'm sorry. I didn't mean to be . . . rude. My head just throbs and throbs — nothing helps. Except when I get up and walk around it feels better. But I'm so tired . . ."

"The water fountain's down there," I said, pointing down one of the halls. "For the Tylenol. I'll show you."

Mrs. Gray followed me.

"I'm so . . . I apologize, Katherine. You were invited here as Jackie's friend and my guest, and I'm just not myself at all. I know Jackie is still angry at me. I thought if you came along and we all had fun that she might . . . ," her voice faltered as she rubbed her temples. We had reached the water fountain but she was just standing there, as if she didn't see it. Gently, I took the Tylenol pack from her hand, ripped it open, and placed the two red and yellow pills in Mrs. Gray's hand.

"Take them," I said.

She did, leaning down and taking a long drink from the fountain. I watched her curiously. Jac had told me once that her mother had been an excellent viola player, and that her dream was to play professionally. But her parents had not supported her ambition and urged her to marry and settle down instead. Jac sometimes felt like giving up the viola had left a deep mark on her mother.

Mrs. Gray finished drinking and straightened.

"You never think . . . ," Mrs. Gray's voice trailed off for a moment. Then she looked at me. "I didn't plan to be this way."

"It's not your fault — something is making your head ache," I said.

She shook her head.

"No. I mean, I didn't plan to be the way that I am. I know your mom isn't like me, Katherine. Jackie talks about her."

I didn't know what to say. I couldn't believe Jac had told her mother everything about my mom, that she was a medium and all that. But Jac did love being at my house, and I guess her mom knew it.

"It's only that I was like Jackie once. It's probably impossible to believe, but I was."

Truthfully, I could hardly believe this *was* Jac's mother. The Mrs. Gray I had known was cool, perfectly put together, and never had much to say to me.

"It's not impossible to believe at all," I said, a little untruthfully. "I think everything is going to be okay, Mrs. Gray. With Jac, with her music, and even with you. She just needs to be in charge sometimes."

There was a silence, and I hoped I hadn't said too much. After a while, Mrs. Gray looked at me. Her eyes seemed to focus on me for the first time.

"I didn't really approve, when you and Jackie became friends," she said.

I gulped silently.

"I didn't want anything or anyone distracting her from her music. But you're a smart girl, Katherine. It's not such a bad thing for Jackie to have you around."

It was kind of a mixed compliment. But it was far and away the nicest thing Jac's mom had ever said to me, so I'd take what I got.

"Thank you," I said. "I'll always look out for her."

Mrs. Gray nodded.

"I'm so tired," she said. "I hate to go back up to that room again, but I can hardly keep my eyes open. I just want to try to sleep. But when I do sleep, I have these dreams."

"Dreams?"

"People chasing me — some shadowy figure with a knife or something. It sounds silly, I know. But they interrupt my sleep. I've missed every parent activity they've offered at this conference so far. I don't want to miss the keynote speaker tonight. Maybe I should go back upstairs and try to take a short nap."

"Oh, don't do that!" I exclaimed.

"Why?"

Good question. Mrs. Gray had only recently decided I wasn't "bad" for Jac. This was not a great time to tell her I suspected a demonic entity was occupying her room. But those dreams . . . a shadowy figure . . . a knife. It was obviously not a coincidence. For whatever reason, Mrs. Gray was attuned to the black cloud. She had a level of psychic ability she wasn't aware of. She was also under a lot of stress. Mrs. Gray seemed to fit the bill of a vulnerable person. I could not let her go back to that room. Not while the thing was still up there.

"My . . . aunt suffers from insomnia," I lied quickly, "and her doctors . . . her sleep specialists always told her the *worst* thing she can do is nap in her bed during the day because her body should associate that bed only with nighttime sleeping. So, if you nap there now, chances are you'll have an even worse time sleeping tonight and the whole cycle will get worse."

"Oh," Mrs. Gray said. "Still, the keynote speaker tonight . . ."

"There's this great reading room on the other side of the lobby, down the hallway with the blue wallpaper. It's got these big comfy chairs and a huge fireplace, and hardly anyone even goes in there. I had a nap there myself. It would probably be very refreshing, just what you need — and you'd feel better for the thing you want to go to tonight. Why don't you try it?"

I don't think Jac's mother really believed what I was saying, or was even listening to me all that closely. It seemed more like she was just so deeply tired she'd do anything to be rid of me. She didn't protest when I took her arm and gently escorted her to the reading room door.

She said nothing, not as I took her to the big comfy chair, and not when I got her settled, waved, and started to walk away.

"Kat?" Mrs. Gray called.

I turned, surprised. Mrs. Gray never used nicknames.

"Thank you."

She looked confused, like she wasn't sure what she was thanking me for.

And it was definitely better that she *not* know.

I smiled at her.

"Any time, Mrs. Gray," I said.

As soon as she settled back into the chair, she looked like she might nod off. I felt it would be safe for her to sleep there. I headed for the stairs. No matter how I felt about the black cloud, I couldn't put off dealing with it any longer. Because it no longer posed a danger just to me — it was threatening Jac's mom as well.

Whatever the black cloud did to me, it had to be overt and aggressive, because I knew where it was and what it was. But Jac's mom only had a vague, subconscious awareness of it. And it seemed from her behavior that the black cloud had already started trying to get into her mind. Given enough time it would probably succeed, and maybe it would start controlling her, the way it had controlled whoever had murdered the girl in 504.

Chapter 18

My room was empty, but I was really jumpy when I went inside. The power was *still* off, and the clouds outside were so thick and black that there was barely any light in my room to see by. I turned all the light switches to the on position, so if the power came back on I would know instantly.

"Madame Serena?" I called.

I sat down on the bed, where I'd been the first time the medium had appeared. But nothing happened.

I sent a short prayer to the Universe, asking it to send me help and protection from any spirit or entity that might wish me harm. My mother had taught me how to do it, but I'd never really felt the need before. I'd been so naïve — assuming that everything out there, in the spirit world or in other dimensions, was ultimately harmless. But the black cloud was anything but harmless.

Worse than that was my realization that this wasn't the only black cloud in the world. I knew for a fact that there was another entity of the same kind, because I'd come face to . . . whatever with it back at school in the library. Presumably that one would come after me again sooner or later, too, and it might even try any time I walked into the library.

I shook my head to clear it. This wasn't the time to think about what was in the library. The mere thought that not one but two demon entities had it in for me was so chilling it took my breath away. Was I so special? Was I such a threat to them? Or did they consider me easy prey?

"Madame Serena," I called. "Madame Serena!"

She didn't come. My thoughts were too scattered, and I was too overtly anxious. I tried to quiet my mind, and broadcast my silent call to her the way I'd done before.

Still nothing. I sat silently, trying to focus even harder. I gave it a good two or three minutes. Then a clap of thunder broke my concentration.

"The thunder bounces off the cliffs. It sounds much louder than it is," came a familiar voice.

She was right where she'd been last time, in full garb, including the turban.

"Madame Serena!" I said, relieved. "You're here!"

"Well, of course I'm here, Simple Cat," she said. "I've been waiting for you ever since we were interrupted by that . . . thing. You have no idea how thrilled I am to be crossing over to the Summerland. You did say you could help me do that, didn't you?"

"Yes, I did say that, Madame Serena, and I can help you. But I need you to help me with something first."

"But, Simple Cat, what could I possibly do for you?" Madame Serena asked, in her strong singsong voice. She sort of reminded me of Glinda the good witch from the *Wizard of Oz*, but older. And taller. And wider.

"I need your help as a medium."

She ducked her head, and squeezed her hands together in her lap.

"I can be of no help to you in that regard, Simple Cat," she said quietly.

"But why not?"

She lifted her head just enough to give me a sad look.

"I've already told you. I never lied, or pretended to my clients. I am *not* a fraud. But I never actually made contact with the spirit world, either. I suppose I wanted to be a medium, because everyone I cared about had crossed over. And there were times when I was alone that I truly believed I could sense spirits. Even see them. But the sad fact I must now face is that I have no abilities of second sight."

"But Madame Serena, you *do*!" I assured her.

She raised one eyebrow, and stared at me, a question in her eyes.

I leaned toward her.

"You said that every time you sensed you were getting through to Loretta, that you would see the black cloud — that it interfered with the connection and you felt forced to end it."

"Yes," Madame Serena said.

"But, Madame Serena, the fact that you could see the black cloud — the fact that it was aware of you — is because you *do* have the second sight. You were never a failure as a medium. The black cloud just interfered with you. And by cutting off the sessions when you sensed it, you actually protected the Colonel's wife."

Madame Serena stared at me intently. Then she leaned over and grasped me by the arms. It didn't feel like a real person was touching me, but I could feel her hands, like two currents of energy.

"Simple Cat, are you certain you are not mistaken?"

I drew myself up theatrically, the way Madame Serena sometimes did.

"Simple Cat is *never* mistaken," I declared. Then I gave her a grin.

She clapped her hands together.

"Then the Colonel's wife had faith in me with good reason! I didn't let her down!"

"You didn't let her down. You kept her safe. And if all goes according to plan, you'll see her soon enough. But, Madame Serena, the black cloud is dangerous to living people. Especially mediums. You know that, don't you?"

She nodded gravely.

"I can affect it," she said. "I can slow it down. But I cannot overpower it."

"And I can stop it from reaching my mind for a time, but I can't overpower it either," I said. "Not by myself. But we can't let that thing remain here. I believe it is responsible for at least one death at the Mountain House. We have to destroy it. I can't do it alone, and neither can you. But together, I think we have a shot of destroying it."

Madame Serena looked sad.

"Simple Cat, I am so fatigued. I never knew how tired I was until you came. I just want to go to the Summerland."

"I know you do," I said. "But you can't let the black cloud stay here. And you can't let all the people who turned on the Spiritualists win."

She gave me an indignant glare.

"How would I be doing that?"

"After Maggie Fox told the newspapers that all of Spiritualism was a fraud, most of the country turned against people like you. They believed that because Maggie claimed to be a fraud, all mediums were."

Madame Serena nodded sadly.

"But you are *not* a fraud," I told her. "And neither am I. I know that you're tired of being here, and you are going to go. You'll be in the Summerland soon. But you have a chance to leave a legacy now, Madame Serena. Even if I'm the only one who knows about it. You can help to rid the Mountain House of this terrible entity. The last act you do on this earth will be to use your abilities to protect innocent people. And wouldn't that be quite the thing for you to tell the Colonel's wife?"

She looked at me for a minute like I was nuts, then she threw back her head and laughed, the way you'd expect an opera singer to laugh — she heaved and quivered, and the sound seemed to reverberate all through the room.

"You are wise, Simple Cat," she said. "It is right for Madame Serena to leave this world with a final gift."

"Okay, then," I said. "When it comes, do

what you can to keep it away from me. It has the ability to push me — to move me, and that terrifies me. I need to keep my mind focused — it feeds off of terror. If I get scared, I'm allowing it to get to me. Can you help?"

Madame Serena drew herself up to her full, impressive height.

"I most certainly can," she declared.

"Okay then. I'm going to try to get its attention."

"How?" Madame Serena asked.

"I guess . . . I'm just going to open myself. As I would to sense any kind of spirit activity. I'm going to broadcast my intent to communicate with the other side."

"Broadcast?" she asked, perplexed.

"Oh, it means . . . never mind. Just sit with me, open your perceptions, take your gaze inward."

"Yes," Madame Serena said, very quietly.

We sat together for a moment, side by side, the sound of our breathing quietly audible over the drum of rainfall.

It seemed barely any time had passed at all when I felt the black cloud's presence — wet and dark and sour.

"It is here," Madame Serena said.

I could see it by the door, swirling darkly. Madame Serena stood up and put herself between us, like a bodyguard. It instantly rose up toward the ceiling, so that I could see it pulsating over the medium's head.

"Dark energy, leave this place," I said, with as much authority as I could gather. I had to pretend I was Madame Serena to muster the commanding tone.

It hung there, menacing.

"In the name of all that is good, in the name of the Divine Guides and all Keepers of Light, I command you to leave this place."

The thing seemed to waver for a moment. Then it began to move toward me.

"Do not approach her," Madame Serena declared loudly. "Comply."

She seemed to be keeping the black cloud in place for the moment, but I could see that she was struggling, and beginning to lose ground. I felt a wave of panic as the thing got a little closer. Fear ate at my stomach, and my hands trembled.

If you let the fear in, you open the door, I told myself. *The black cloud feeds on terror.*

Madame Serena cried out and staggered back, as if she'd been shoved. The cloud glided closer.

Orin had told me to hit the thing with an image of what I loved most in the world.

I closed my eyes and blotted out everything in the room, and replaced it.

With the face of my mother.

I thought of the sensation of her rubbing my back. The smell of her cookies baking. The sound of her laughter. I thought of her reverence for all forms of life — the way she carried spiders outside of the house, and wouldn't even kill wasps. I thought of the way she offered help to others no matter who they were. And I thought of the way she cared for me, the ways she always had and would.

Then I let myself feel the love I had inside for her — I felt it expand and surge far beyond the confines of my body.

"In the name of light, *be gone*!" I heard Madame Serena shout as she staggered back toward me.

Something ripped through me, tearing

me open down the middle. Then I felt a sense of enormous space, like gravity had released its pull and I was tumbling into the sky. The floor hit me hard, knocking the breath out of me. The entity seemed to be sucked into itself like a black hole, until it was completely gone.

And the room was flooded with light.

Chapter 19

At first I thought I was alone in the room, as I sat on the floor trying to regain my senses. I didn't know how long the power had been back on, but the lights were working now. Everything seemed too bright. Then I caught sight of Madame Serena's turban peeking over the foot of the bed. Then two bejeweled hands grasped the footboard, and she pulled herself up.

"I do believe, Simple Cat, that we were successful," she declared, straightening her turban solemnly.

I started to stand, but felt kind of wobbly, so I perched on the end of the bed. The energy in the room was totally different — though the sky was still dark outside the room felt as sunny and warm as a beach on a bright July afternoon.

"You're right," I said. "You're right! Madame Serena, we did it!"

She pressed her hand to her chest, as she always did when she was feeling emotional. Her eyes filled with tears. A strand of iron gray hair hung down from beneath the turban, and she tucked it behind one ear.

"Thank you, Simple Cat," she said. "It is so meaningful . . . to know that I made a difference before I departed."

"You did," I told her earnestly. "I couldn't have done it without you. I would never have even tried."

A tear spilled out of one eye and rolled

down her wrinkled face. When it reached her lip, she smiled.

"You want to go now, don't you?" I asked her.

I almost wished she'd say no. Madame Serena was one of my people. I wouldn't have minded spending some quality time with her, now that the black cloud was gone.

"I do, Simple Cat. I want to go — more than anything."

"I'll try to help with that now. Come sit next to me," I said. "Facing the window."

She sat down obediently, her phantom form making an impressive dent on the mattress. I'd never actually helped a spirit cross over. Suzanne Bennis at school had done it herself. The ghosts at the house next to mine had needed a different kind of help. But my mother had told me many stories of how she'd helped spirits who had accepted their deaths leave the physical dimension for good. I had a general idea how it worked. Still, I felt a little nervous. After all this, what if Madame Serena was still stuck here with me?

"Relax and breathe," I told her. "Follow the breath, nothing but the breath. In. Out. In. Out."

Her chest rose and fell, and the room felt very silent and serene.

"Try and release your connection to this place. Tell yourself it's okay to go now. Tell yourself you've done what you needed to do."

Her lips moved silently.

I waited.

"Do you see anything?" I asked her. She opened her eyes, and shook her head.

"Is something wrong?" Madame Serena asked. "What am I supposed to see?"

Heck if I knew.

"You're doing fine," I said. "Everything

is fine. Um, direct your senses outward, like you would when you were trying to reach Loretta for the Colonel's wife."

Madame Serena nodded.

"Visualize a . . . a door," I said.

I really hoped I was going in the right direction here.

"I see the door," Madame Serena said.

"You do?" I asked. "I mean, yes, you do and you can reach out and . . . open it."

There was silence for a moment, then Madame Serena nodded excitedly.

"Yes! It's open!"

"Do you . . . see anything through the door?" I asked.

"Light. It's very bright through the door," she said.

"That's right," I said, relieved. "That's right. And the light can see you, too. Talk to it. Ask for the light to come through to you,

Madame Serena. Call to the light, and tell it you are ready to cross over."

"Light of Summerland, I ask you come to me now. I am ready to leave this place. I am ready to render myself unto your grace."

Oh good. She said it much better than I could have. And something must be working because her face was lit with a glorious smile. Actually, her face was lit with... light.

I turned toward where the window had been. I gasped. Sun seeped through a rectangular outline. Nothing, not even my mother's descriptions, could have prepared me for this. It was warm and golden and alive — I could sense a deep and loving intelligence coming from inside it. I wanted to laugh and sob at the same time.

As I stared at the rectangle of light, transfixed, a figure appeared just inside it.

"The Colonel's wife," whispered Madame Serena. "She's come to guide me over!"

Sure enough, I could now see the figure was a woman, short and slender with gray hair and a pleasant face. She was cradling something in her arms, holding it close to her heart.

Madame Serena got to her feet.

"Is it . . . oh my dear, have you brought Loretta?"

The woman smiled and nodded. Light seemed to be coming out of her, too. She walked to the very edge of the doorway, so that it seemed she was standing both in the light and in the room just in front of us.

Still holding Loretta close to her chest, the Colonel's wife raised her other hand, and beckoned for Madame Serena to come toward her.

"It's okay," I told her. "Go, Madame Serena."

She turned and looked at me, her eyes clear and bright. She reached up and pulled her turban off, and let it drop to the floor. Beautiful silver hair tumbled out, long and wavy and falling well below her shoulders. As I watched her, the hair seemed to change from gray to blond. The wrinkles and lines began to fade from her face. Her waist began to melt until she was as slender as a girl. I was stunned. Did this happen to everyone? Madame Serena looked no older than me! Maybe she was reverting to the last age she was really happy.

"Thank you, Simple Cat," she said. "I will watch over you. If you ever need me, I will be listening for your call."

I smiled and nodded, too emotional to

say anything. What I was witnessing was so mind-boggling I could hardly breathe.

Madame Serena took several steps. She was at the very edge of the light, and then she was in it. She stood next to the Colonel's wife, and gazed down at Loretta, smiling.

Unable to stop myself, I took a few steps toward them. They were both smiling at me. I looked down at the little bundle in the arms of the Colonel's wife — and got a quick glimpse at the face of Loretta.

Then it all faded out very suddenly — like someone had switched off a television. I was looking out and through the window now, at the lake and the cliffs facing the Mountain House. The room was absolutely silent. Even the rain had stopped.

I sat heavily down on the bed. Speechless. I don't know what affected me the most. We had defeated the black cloud. The light had come. Madame Serena had been greeted by the Colonel's wife, and had crossed over to the other side.

I had seen the face of Loretta, whose death had so devastated the Colonel's wife.

And Loretta was a dog.

Chapter 20

"A pug?"

"A very cute pug."

"Loretta was a *pug*?" Orin's laugh permeated his words. "That is a new one on me."

I laughed too, happy and comfortable in a large Adirondack chair on the Mountain House porch. The sun was peeking through the clouds, and the lake gleamed. I switched my cell phone to the other ear.

"I know, right? But anyway, I still can't get my mom, and I wanted to give you the heads-up that it's all okay now. I had to re-charge my cell phone, and now that it works she's still not picking up. But the entity is gone, and everything is fine."

Orin made a dismayed sound.

"What?"

"Well, I told you I was going over to your house," Orin said. "She was there, out in the garden. She was pretty freaked out about the entity."

"What? But I'm okay!" I said.

"She tried to call your cell, and it was turned off," Orin said.

"The battery," I said glumly.

"So she tore off to help you."

"She tore off to where?"

As soon as I said it, the very instant the words were out of my mouth, an old brown car rounded the corner of the Mountain

House drive. I'd know that 1994 Chevy with the dinged front bumper and the crooked windshield wipers anywhere.

"Never mind, I think I know the answer to that. I'll talk to you later, Orin."

I snapped the phone shut as he was saying good-bye.

All I could think was I had to get her attention. I didn't want her to spend one more minute thinking something terrible had happened to me. The Mountain House was at least fifty miles from where we lived; she must have driven like a madwoman to get here on the back mountain roads in under two hours.

I ran down the steps, waving with one hand, and flashing a thumbs-up with the other. A group of three conservatively dressed middle-aged women unpacking their red SUV gave me a curious, disapproving look. I blasted past them as the Chevy rounded the corner into the circular unloading zone. She screeched to a halt behind the SUV and leapt out of the car.

"I'm fine, I'm fine," I said, even as she was grabbing me and pulling me into a hug.

"Kat, Orin said . . ."

"I know, but it's all over, and I'm fine," I repeated.

I'd never seen my mother look truly frightened. Her pale blue eyes were wide, her eyebrows furrowed, and her baby-fine blond hair was coming out of a hastily made ponytail. There was a time I thought nothing in the known world could scare my mother. But now I knew that I could.

"What Orin said . . . that thing could really hurt you," she said, holding me at arm's length and examining me, like she was looking for marks.

"But it didn't," I said. "And it's gone now. I'll tell you exactly what happened, Mom, but I'd love to not talk about it just yet. It's really gone. I just sort of need some . . . distance from it."

She nodded. The fear was beginning to leave her face, but she was still frowning.

"You're okay," she stated.

I nodded. She tucked a strand of hair behind one ear, and sighed. She was still wearing her gardening clothes — ancient baggy denim overalls and an orange tank top. Smudges of dirt decorated her knees and hands.

The SUV ladies were still standing there, watching us openly as if they'd bought tickets to a show. The bellboy was waiting for them to notice him so he could take their luggage. When I noticed the ladies staring at my mother, I hugged her tight.

"I am *so* glad you're here," I said loudly. Then I glanced over at the audience and flashed them a ridiculous, over-the-top grin, shooting my eyebrows up and down. They quickly pretended they hadn't been watching us, and one of them began issuing detailed suitcase-handling instructions to the bellboy.

"I shouldn't be here, though," my mom said. "This is your time with Jac and her mom. I just needed to get to you, in case . . . but you're okay."

I grinned.

"I. Am. Okay."

"That's all I needed to know," she said. "I should get back."

"Mom, come on, you just got here!" I cried. "At least have a look around — it's amazing! There's a labyrinth out back that's haunted by a cute little girl with a kitten —

and there's a huge reading room and a trail up to the fire tower . . ."

She smiled at me, and looked up at the enormous front face of the Mountain House.

"I don't really think I belong here," she said quietly.

I grabbed her hand.

"Ridiculous," I declared. "*I'm* here, and that means you belong here, too."

She allowed me to lead her down to the little bench by the lake where Jac and I had first seen Colin, the Virtuoso Worm Boy.

"How *is* Jac?" my mom asked. "You haven't mentioned her at all."

"We're kind of not getting along," I said. Then I gave her a summary of what had happened. I left out the part about being accused of kissing up to Mrs. Gray in the hopes of being included on vacations my own mother couldn't afford.

"Oh, Kat, I'm so sorry," my mom said. "You have to know that what's going on with Jac is not about you, right?"

"No, I know. It just doesn't help all that much."

"No," my mom agreed. "But from everything I know about Jac, I think you're right on the mark — this is all about the cello, and her mother. She wants to go back to the cello for real, but she doesn't want to give her mother the satisfaction. She's got to let go of her anger at her mother — she has to want to stop punishing her. Because it's preventing her from following her heart. Nothing is going to go right for Jac until she gets that straight."

"That's basically just what I told her, and

all it did was make her furious. She accused me of being allied with her mother!"

"Kat, you've done everything possible," my mom said gently. "There's only one thing left to do."

"What?" I asked eagerly.

"Nothing. You have to just wait, and do nothing. Just be there. I know Jac's making it really difficult for you, but just try to be there as her friend. No one would blame you if you just threw in the towel, abandoned Jac, and asked me to take you home right now. Which I will, if you want. But I truly think she'll come around, Kat. I know she will. And if you're there waiting for her when she does, that makes your friendship all the stronger. Jac is worth the long haul. And in spite of all this, she's as good a friend to you as you are to her."

Just to have someone, just one person,

understand my position made all the difference in the world. Just hearing confirmation that yes, you've been treated badly and yes, you have a right to be mad, and sure, you have every right to give up and go — that gave me the patience I needed to stay.

"I actually feel better already," I said. "It's going to be fine. And seriously, Mom, isn't this place spectacular? Even with Jac not really speaking to me, I'm kind of having a decent time! Don't you want to come see my room?"

"I'm going to head back, sweetie. I left all my stuff out in the garden, and Max is going to need to be walked. Now that I've seen you, I'll be fine. Save the details for when you get home."

"Okay."

"I love you, Kat. And listen, I'm really proud of you."

I looked at her curiously. The ponytail had come out completely, and her hair was blowing softly around her face. Her eyes had softened.

"For what?"

"You're making some difficult choices, and you're seeing them through. You helped a spirit cross over. You went head-to-head with something . . . terrible. Something that most mediums wouldn't touch for anything in the world. And in spite of the fact that you like to do things on your own, without help, you called Orin for help when your intuition told you that you might be in over your head. You did exactly the right thing."

"I couldn't have gotten through it without the information he gave me, without his advice," I said.

"Yeah. He's a really wise guy. We owe him one heck of a dinner."

I smiled, and looked at my feet.

"And that's not even all, Kat. I'm also proud because you tried to help your best friend and got blasted for it, and you're sticking around anyway. You're there for her. You are an old soul, my love. I've always known it."

"Takes one to know one," I told her.

She squeezed my shoulder, then stood up.

"Walk me to my car?" she asked.

"Sure, if they haven't towed it away," I said.

She laughed.

"It does stand out a bit, doesn't it?" she asked, shaking her head.

"That's okay, Mom," I assured her. "I stand out, too. And really, I don't mind. I'm actually sort of starting to like it."

The crazy thing is, it was true.

Chapter 21

I remembered to check at the front desk on my way to dinner, and as promised, Alex had left me a book. It was the slim biography of Maggie Fox, titled *The Unhappy Medium.* I carried it in to dinner with me. Since I'd probably be eating alone, I might as well have something to read.

I examined the cover as I walked to the dining hall. It was decorated with an oval photograph of the unhappy medium herself. Maggie Fox was very pretty, with thick dark hair, large and expressive brown eyes, and a girlishly round face.

That could have been me, I thought. If I had been born in another time, another place. I could have been that girl, sought out by thousands and made famous by virtue of the dead. Thrust into the limelight as a teenager. How would I have reacted?

I chose to eat in the casual dining room where Jac and I had gone our first night at the Mountain House. Because there were no grown-ups to admonish me, I made myself a plate consisting mostly of mashed potatoes, with a smattering of lima beans as a token acknowledgement of the vegetable world. To me, there was nothing in the world as comforting as a large helping of mashed potatoes dripping in butter. I rounded the meal out with a sixteen-ounce glass of root beer. No ice. It was about as far from the nutrition pyramid as a meal was likely to get, and I was thrilled with it.

I tucked into my dinner and my book with great enthusiasm. Now that my ordeal was over, I wanted to know more about the mysterious leader of the Spiritualists. Everything around me faded as I entered Maggie Fox's world, from the first recorded episodes where she and her sister Katy stunned their family with spirit rappings.

The giddy teenage girls gave way to mysterious young women, as the pair, urged on by their ambitious older sister Leah, toured the country charging for their spirit sessions. When I began to read about Maggie's secret love affair with a dashing Arctic explorer who was considered a national hero, I was utterly hooked. But something made me look up.

Jac noticed me the same time I noticed

her. I was all the way in the corner, with my back mostly to the door. She had come in and taken a seat just by the door. Our eyes met at the same moment. She looked surprised and dismayed. I'm sure I did, too.

"Colin asked me to have dinner with him," she said after a minute. She looked at her feet as she spoke. "We arranged to meet here, on this porch. So I . . ."

"It's fine," I said. "I'm just about done. I'll be out of your hair."

There was an uncomfortable silence. It was the first time since I'd met Jac at the beginning of the school year that we had nothing to say to each other. I picked up my book and ducked my head, relieved to have something to do. But I couldn't read. I just stared at the type on the page.

I should just get up and leave, I thought. *This is ridiculous.*

And I was planning to do just that, when Colin walked onto the porch.

With his arm around the Barbie girl.

"Yo, wassup, Cello Genius?" he asked Jac.

God, I loathed it when boys like Colin tried to use expressions like *yo* and *wassup*. It was so . . . pathetic.

Jac was frozen. I could see that her fists were tightly clenched in her lap. Colin must have felt my stare, because he looked over at me.

"Yo, honorary musician. Oh man, is that root beer? I could use one of those right about now."

"I'll get one for you," said the Barbie. And she shot Jac a look that was not nice at all.

"That's my Cleo," Colin said.

I almost snorted with laughter. Cleo was as plastic as they came.

Jac had gone absolutely rigid. I knew her

body language, and I knew all her expressions. She was trying with every ounce of energy she had not to cry.

"So what's goin' on, Jac?" Colin asked.

Either this guy was a genuine bully, or he was the stupidest human ever to learn a musical instrument. Didn't he know that Jac was crushing on him? Didn't he know that he'd given her the impression they were an item?

I stood up, my drink in hand, and walked over to Colin. I stood very close to him, and looked him right in the eye.

"You're a lot shorter than I realized," I said, in the same pleasant, conversational tone he'd used with Jac. "That must be tough. I guess the violin thing helps compensate, right? I'm sure that helps the . . . you know."

Colin looked very confused, like he

couldn't believe I was really insulting him —
that it was a misunderstanding.

"Helps the what?" he asked.

I glanced dramatically to the right and
left, like Madame Serena, as if I wanted to
make sure no one could overhear. Then I
leaned forward and whispered as loud as I
could.

"The Napoleon thing. You know, a male's
obsessive rage at his short stature. I once
had a teacher who had it."

Then I offered him my root beer.

"Sip?" I asked.

"You need to back off," he said, with a
scowl.

I shrugged and smiled sweetly.

"I don't know, Colin. That's an awfully
tall order."

Colin uttered some indiscernible exclamation of rage and stormed out before Cleo returned with his root beer.

And Jac got up.

For a moment, I had the dreadful impression that I'd made a mistake — that by humiliating Colin I'd made Jac even madder at me.

But then she threw her arms around me.

"You are my best friend in the entire world," she said.

And then she burst into tears.

Chapter 22

We had made a nice nest in my bed, which was more than large enough for the two of us, our books, Jac's beloved and bedraggled stuffed beagle Milo, and a big box of malted milk balls. Jac had stopped crying some time ago, but her eyes were still puffy and her nose was still red.

"And so then, when that girl and what's-his-name were arguing about which way the trail went, he kept giving me these smiles, right?"

I nodded and offered the box of malted

milk balls to Jac. She popped two in her mouth and they pooched out her cheeks, making her look like a depressed chipmunk. She clutched Milo to her heart.

"And then he took my hand, Kat — he took my hand! And held it! And he said, 'I'm really glad you're here, Jac. You're an amazing girl.' Now, that's not a signal that can get mixed, right?"

I shook my head.

"Because if you hold somebody's hand and tell them they're amazing, that's like, boyfriend-girlfriend talk. Isn't it?"

"Absolutely," I said emphatically. "Totally."

"Right! So then this afternoon when I went to the strings and woodwinds symposium, he was rushing out the door just as I was getting there. And he said he'd broken two strings on his violin and had the wrong ones in his case, and that he had to go find new strings to replace them. And I was like, fine, and then he put his arm around me and said, 'But let's have dinner tonight, Jac — what do you say?' Wouldn't you think that was a date?"

"Of course I would. Anyone would!" I said, handing her the box of malted milk balls again. This time she waved it away.

"I just feel so . . . stupid. To think a guy like Colin would . . . I mean, it's so humiliating, Kat! Did you see that look Cleo shot at me? How could I have thought for a minute that he'd go for somebody like me over somebody like her?"

"Because any sane guy would!" I exclaimed. "And because he deliberately made you think he liked you. He's a jerk, Jac. He messes around with girls' feelings because it makes him feel better about himself."

Jac sniffed and peered into the candy box like the truth might be in there.

"Do you really think so?" she asked. "You think he was messing with me on purpose?"

"I'm sure he was," I declared. "You weren't imagining anything, Jac. The guy played you. I'm not saying he was making fun of you — I think he really did like you. I think he did want to hold your hand. The problem is, I think he felt the same way about Cleo, and about who knows who else. A guy like that doesn't see any problem going after all the girls he likes at the same time, and making them think they're the only one. And he's going to rack up some major bad karma treating people that way."

"Cleo's not even a very good clarinet player," Jac said. "For real. I don't know how she got accepted to the conference. Except I heard her dad has major bucks."

"Well, there aren't many places in the world you can't buy your way into," I said. "Not that I know from personal experience."

Jac gave me a long look.

"You really are unbelievable," she said.

Uh-oh. What now?

"Huh?" I asked, grabbing the box back. I might need the power and support of milk chocolate if we were going to fight again.

"I have been a huge selfish cow ever since we got here, and I've been awful to you. It was bad enough I had to obsess over . . . him, but then . . . in the boat today. Kat, I didn't mean any of those things I said to you. The reason I got so angry was because everything you said was right. It was kind of eerie — like you could see right into my mind."

"I can't, if it makes you feel any better," I told her gently. "I just know you really well, Jac. You're like my sister."

"And you're like mine!" she cried. "And you do know me really well. I *am* ready to go back to the cello. I want to study again, I want to perform. I want to come to conferences and hang out with other young musicians. Some of them, anyway. And the thing you were rightest about, the thing that really made me flip out, was that I didn't want my mother to think she'd won."

"But she didn't win, Jac," I said quietly. "And she knows it. You won. Because you get to follow your dream, and she had to give hers up. Imagine how *that* must feel. You've always assumed she pushes your music to control you. But maybe she pushes you so you can have what she couldn't."

Jac hung her head.

"Yeah," she murmured. "It's hard for me to think of her like that, you know."

"Like what?" I asked.

"Like a person. I think of her as my mother. Reason for All Pain. But she's got her own pain, I guess."

I held the box of malted milk balls out to her.

"Why don't you bring her a peace offering? Nothing tastes better with a glass of Fiji water than a nice crunchy malted milk ball."

Jac grinned, and took the box.

"Okay," she said, getting out of bed. "But she better only take one."

Long after Jac had fallen asleep next to me, I lay in bed reading about the life of Maggie Fox. It was really tragic.

She had met and fallen in love with the famous Arctic explorer, Elisha Kent Kane. He sent her letter upon letter declaring the depths of the love he had for her, and vowing his intention to make her his wife. All he asked was that she give up her Spiritualism and her séances, which he felt went against God.

Head over heels in love with him, Maggie agreed. But the Kane family was wealthy and powerful, and they refused to allow their son to marry a poor girl who had made her name conducting spirit sessions. Kane left on a two-year expedition to the Arctic, and when he returned, he told Maggie he was forced to end their engagement. Her heart was broken, and she suffered a devastating breakdown.

Kane never seemed to be able to make up his mind. They were back together again, then not. Then he showed up one day, and with her mother as a witness, he "married" Maggie, with the two stating their vows to each other. Shortly afterward, Kane took sick and died.

The shock of it almost killed Maggie. To make things worse, the Kanes refused to acknowledge that the marriage had happened. They claimed Maggie was a simple and unstable woman and had invented the whole thing. Maggie never fully recovered.

What I found most interesting was that according to the book, a year after her famous "confession," Maggie recanted, as Alex Kenyon had told me. It was the confession, Maggie announced, that had been the falsehood. Maggie then resumed her Spiritualist activities. But by this time no one trusted her. She died penniless and almost entirely alone.

The doctor that attended to her on her deathbed found that she was almost completely paralyzed. She could move neither her hands or her feet. And yet, the doctor reported, when he tended to her the room erupted with the sound of rapping — on the floor, the wall, and the ceiling.

So which was the truth? I supposed that no one could ever know. The truth had died with Maggie Fox. What I did know was from the moment she'd turned her back on who she was, everything in her life had gone wrong. That made me think of Jac.

I closed the book, and leaned down to place it on the floor. My hand brushed on something soft poking out from under the bed. I picked it up and held it near the light.

It was Madame Serena's turban.

I smiled, tucked it under my pillow, and turned out the light. And for the first time since I'd arrived at the Whispering Pines Mountain House, I got an absolutely peaceful night's sleep.

Chapter 23

"Are you sure you packed enough energy bars?" Jac asked anxiously.

"Jac, it's a three-hour hike max, round trip," I told my friend, looking at her affectionately.

Jac's own backpack was crammed with sunblock, anti-bug cream, anti-sting stuff, anti-tick spray, anti–poison ivy lotion, and a pocket transmitter that emitted a high-frequency sound, inaudible to human ears but said to keep wildlife away.

"We need some kind of locating beacon," she said. "You know, for if we get lost."

I held up my cell phone.

"Got one right here," I told her. "Jac, it's a hike up to the mountaintop, not the Apollo 13 mission to the moon."

"I can't believe I let you talk me into this," she said. "I could be at the Baroque Brunch right now."

I paused and looked at my friend, who was sitting cross-legged on the wide porch of the Mountain House, rifling through her backpack.

"Do you want to be?" I asked. "Seriously, Jac, if that's one of the programs you want to go to, we could do the hike another —"

Jac swatted at me with one of the trail maps she'd collected.

"That was a *joke*," she said, rolling her

eyes. "There's no Baroque Brunch — I made it up. Some psychic you are, Voodoo Mama."

"I'm not a psychic, I'm a medium," I said primly. "Well, if we're going, let's go! Zip that pack closed, Maestra."

She obeyed, and with a little difficulty got the pack on. She stood up, bounced a few times on the balls of her feet, and gave me the thumbs-up. "I'm ready!"

I chuckled quietly as I put my own pack on. For the first time since we'd come to the Mountain House, Jac and I had scheduled an entire morning to hang out together. It was a gorgeous day, and my heart was wide open and full of light.

"Lead on, Macduff," Jac declared.

We walked down the steps from the front porch of the Mountain House, and began to trudge over the gravel drive toward the Skytop Trail. There was a family in the drop-off circle loading up their belongings. It looked like they'd been at the Mountain House for weeks, from the looks of their luggage. Several Whispering Pines employees were chatting up the mother and father, and all at once I noticed that one of them was Ted Kenyon. And oh man, standing right next to him was Alex. They both saw me at the same time and waved, then glanced at each other in surprise.

"Hey, give me a sec, okay?" I asked Jac.

She raised one eyebrow at me, and then she nodded.

I walked toward the Kenyons, who separated themselves from the group and came over to me.

"Hi Alex," I said. Then realizing I couldn't avoid Ted, I glanced at him and said, "and Ted."

"I see you already know my son," Alex said with a sly smile.

Oh, for the love of Pete. I totally should have known. It was la-dee-duh coming back to haunt me.

"Yep," I said quickly, anxious to move away from that subject. "So I read the book you left for me, Alex — *The Unhappy Medium.* It was amazing!"

I tried not to notice Ted's expression — he looked for the moment like the Unhappy Kenyon. It must be awkward discovering I knew his mom. Maybe he wondered what I'd told her about him.

"You liked it, huh?" Alex said.

"Loved it. And I have a theory."

"Let me hear it," Alex said, sounding delighted.

Ted looked down at his feet, shifting his

weight from side to side. He looked much better out here in the sunlight — his squatness translated to muscle, and his Cro-Magnon brow looked slightly noble.

"I think Maggie's first confession was the fake one. I think she brooded about Elisha Kent Kane for years and years, and because it had been so important to him that she give up being a medium, and renounce Spiritualism, she made the confession for him after his death. Because she couldn't get over him, and it was the only way she could connect to him. But then, after a year, she couldn't live with not being herself anymore. Because she'd been a medium longer than she'd loved Elisha Kent Kane. In the end, she wanted her identity back. So she told the truth the second time — she really was a medium. And that's my theory."

"That is *precisely* the conclusion I came to," Alex said. "I love that you're interested in all this stuff."

Ted was still staring at his shoes.

"Well, Ted really helped to get me curious about the Spiritualist history," I said. "He lent me a Mountain House scrapbook, from 1888."

Ted looked up at me like he'd given up hope I was going to acknowledge him.

"It was a really interesting scrapbook," I said. "I don't think I got a chance to thank you."

"No, I was glad to . . . get it for you."

Ted's feet were apparently quite fascinating, because he resumed looking at them.

"Well, I have a question. For either of you, or both of you. Wasn't someone murdered in room 504 that year, 1888?"

Ted's mouth dropped open, and his mother laughed.

"Ouch. You've found one of the skeletons in our closet," Alex said, but she sounded far more amused than concerned.

"Do you know anything about it?" I asked.

"A little bit," Alex said. "It was a young woman from Massachussetts, as I recall. Traveling alone, no family. Killed in her room well after midnight. Stabbed, as I recall it."

Definitely stabbed.

"And they never caught who did it?" I asked.

Alex glanced at her son.

"Oh, they caught him all right. He was staying in the room across the hall from hers."

My room.

"There was a theory at the time that they were actually meeting at the hotel — that perhaps they were sweethearts, planning on running off together. And then something happened. And he killed her. Turned himself in the next morning. Young man by the name of Philip Kenyon."

"Kenyon?"

"One of the cousins," Ted said. "That's why that part of it was hushed up. The Kenyons had a lot of influence locally in those days. They couldn't sweep the murder totally under the rug, but they kept cousin Philip's name out of the papers."

"There was part of an article in the scrapbook," I said. "Just the headline and a few sentences — the rest had been ripped out."

"Granny strikes again," Ted said, and Alex gave a hoot of laughter.

"My mother-in-law," she told me. "The year she married into the Kenyon family, she went through all the scrapbooks and tore out anything even remotely unpleasant. That's why almost no one today knows what happened. Which reminds me — how did you know it was room 504? I didn't think anyone had that detail but family."

I smiled cryptically.

"Just a hunch," I said.

"One heck of a hunch," Ted said, giving me a very curious look.

Jac had been slowly edging toward us, and now she stepped up to my elbow and cleared her throat.

"This is my friend Jac," I said. "Ted Kenyon, and his mom Alex Kenyon."

"The one that —," Jac began.

I stepped firmly on Jac's foot.

"We're going to hike Skytop," I said.

"Oh, that's a great hike," Ted said. "You can see for miles in every direction up there."

"You should show your friend the labyrinth, too," Alex said, a twinkle in her eyes. She leaned toward me.

"You know, since you're learning all our secrets anyway, the labyrinth annex is supposed to be haunted."

"Is it really?" I said, pretending to look surprised. From the way Alex was looking at me, I wondered just how much she'd guessed about me.

"Yeah, by a little girl. The daughter of a maid. The child died of influenza in 1915 or '16, I think. The labyrinth annex was her favorite place. They say you can see her skipping through it sometimes, holding something . . . a doll, I think it might have been, or . . ."

"A kitten," I said innocently.

Alex's eyebrows shot up.

"Now that you mention it, I think it was a kitten."

"Well, we should get going," I said. "Are you ready, Jac?"

"Well, if the labyrinth is haunted, I want to go there," Jac declared.

"No way you're getting out of this hike. We'll go later. Bye!"

I waved to Ted and then to Alex, who was standing and staring at me with a half smile on her face.

Jac and I were walking toward the path when Ted called after me.

"Kat?"

I turned around.

"If you want, give me your e-mail address. I mean, if you're still interested in the Spiritualists. Or anything. I could send stuff to you. Or my mom could."

I grinned.

"My e-mail address is MediumGirl @nowmail.com," I told him.

And without waiting for his or his mother's reaction, I turned on my heel and departed.

That is my real e-mail address, by the way.

Jac and I talked about everything under the sun as we trudged up the wide and pine-needle carpeted trail. It was like our fight had never happened, but better. I was really excited about getting to the top and seeing the view that Ted had mentioned. I loved seeing things from a different perspective. There was always something you could see clearly that you had never noticed before, even though it had been there all along.

Who knew — by the time we reached the top, I might even be ready to tell Jac her mom had a touch of the second sight.

I was keeping my options open, though.